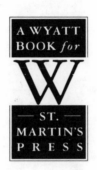

A WYATT BOOK *for*

W

— ST. —
MARTIN'S
PRESS

VISITATION

DON CUSHMAN

For Dean
Ron

A Wyatt Book for St. Martin's Press ❧
New York

Design by Junie Lee

Library of Congress Cataloging-in-Publication Data

Cushman, Don.
    Visitation / by Don Cushman.—1st ed.
      p.   cm.
    "A Wyatt book for St. Martin's Press."
    ISBN 0-312-14062-2
    I. Title.
    PS3553.U74V57   1996   95-41356
    813.54—dc20   CIP

First Edition: February 1996

10 9 8 7 6 5 4 3 2 1

To JoAnn Ugolini, my wife,
whose love, understanding, and support
sustain me

I would like to thank Kathleen Fraser for her editorial assistance and encouragement, and Michele Bloom and Lisa Warhuus, my daughters, for being faithful and loving readers.

VISITATION

CHAPTER ONE

Siena. In my meditations, which I freely admit are now more Buddhist than Augustinian, I go back through the cultured streets, scurry up the steps and into the cathedral. My bones rattling as though I carried them in a sack, I make my way over the mosaics to the spot that is my madness and my cure.

The mystery begins here on the floor, which is no longer cold in my feverish prostrations. The mosaic of the wheel of fortune. The man is the same man at every stage. But still the wheel takes him to the heights of hope—yes, ecstasy—then dashes him into abandonment and despair. You must understand me. What place does the wheel have in the house of God? How could an all-knowing and wise deity devise the rack of time to turn of its own inexorable energy and so, without reason, take me from the giddy promontories of expectation to the depths of shame and self-loathing?

The man is the same. He has the same pool of talents, the same body, mind, the same breath of life whistling through him. He is the same in the sight of God. Yet he suffers regardless of his efforts, regardless of his spiritual advancement to satisfy the hideous machine of time.

I do not mean to begin at the beginning. I do not mean to begin at all. I do not mean to describe my time on the rack. I am urged on by unseen hands, rudely pushed to record, no, not to record, but to revenge myself against time.

I who now labor in a purgatory of purgatories, I who

now work in the secret rooms of a secret library from where no light escapes, speak to you from farther than the grave. For the grave is a release from time, no matter what punishment or ecstasy ensues, and I am the prisoner of time, left with my memories to torture me into silence. And it is the truth that has kept me silent and refused to release me.

It begins in a seminary set in the lush California hills. Vines swept down the hills. I walked among them at peace. The harvest a success, rest beckoned from the empty tendrils. My dissertation was finished and in the hands of my superiors. Had I knowledge, I would have heard in the distance the slight tremors of the wheel beginning its slow ascent. The sun was already over the oaks and soon the bats would be whirling overhead like aerial dervishes. I walked among the vines, my thoughts as muted as the light. And I watched a line of dust move toward me down the hill. The old truck shuddered to a stop and a voice shouted to me over the engine noise, "Gabriel, Clanahan wants to see you."

I should have kept walking. I should at least have heard the wheel click into the next notch. I got into the truck and we crawled back up the hill in low gear, my mind racing around the grounds.

I ran up the marble staircase, past an imitation Matisse banner that was popular with nuns that year, paused a few heartbeats, then knocked on Rector Patrick C. Clanahan's exquisitely overcarved door. It had always meant abandoning some kind of hope to cross that threshold. At that moment I didn't have enough to abandon, so it was with confusion and not contrition that I entered.

His office was ostentatious without purpose. It was filled with endless volumes of canon law, the color purple, and a desk with not quite enough oak to build a trireme. It was meant to instill awe. We always referred to it as the "holy of holies."

Monsignor Clanahan was a rock of a man, a rock to

run aground against, not build upon. He had a granite jaw, tobacco-stained teeth, and an unearthly pallor no one mistook for saintliness. He had been second or third in the running for a bishopric until rumors of his drinking and a $200,000 shortfall in his parish books undid him. He had just enough pull left to end his days as rector of the diocesan seminary. He drank enough scotch to keep the bile from choking him and took his revenge on everyone who crossed the lintel.

"Father D'Amato," he wheezed through his whiskeyed afternoon as he fixed me with his implacable stare, "it seems you have been discovered. Your paper has rung some distant chimes. Why, I can't say. I read some of it and don't understand a damn word. What I do understand verges on blasphemy. But it has landed on fertile soil. Rome, I hear. Your name echoes in the sacrosanct porticoes of the Vatican. I told them you were a young cleric with little promise and even less piety, that your scholarship must be mostly plagiarism, that you put your colleagues to sleep and confuse your students. But, apparently, they have heard otherwise.

"You seem to be needed in Rome. 'New blood,' they say. More like fresh blood. So you're off to suckle at the teats that nourished Romulus and Remus. But, Father D'Amato, don't forget for a minute that it is still a she-wolf no matter how sweet the milk.

"You're to tell everyone that you're there to participate in an ecumenical conference. In reality you are to report to a very secret organization of scholars. So secret I wasn't given its name or purpose.

"I do not have the ear of the See. What Rome wants is always a mystery, but you had better not disgrace the name of this institution or I will be the hound at your heels. You have some packing to do, Father." He handed me a manila envelope with the Vatican's ornate seal and dismissed me with a look that destroyed any question I might have had.

Clanahan's appraisal of me keeps echoing in the background of my meditations. I considered myself superior to the broken and exiled rector. I was destined for Rome and he for the clerical scrapheap. Why should I have listened?

Are you surprised to hear such unchristian attitudes from a cleric? Don't be. We had been stuffed like geese headed for foie gras with poverty, humility, charity, agape, and other forgotten virtues, while the real virtues were more corporate: ambition, prejudice, and unscrupulous attitudes hidden behind masks of innocence. The saintly had been cut from the fold before they became priests. They had the habit of developing ambivalent attitudes toward certain Church teachings when faced with the pain those teachings caused their parishioners.

The saintly had embarrassing and costly nervous breakdowns. Wise rectors found ways to expel them from the seminary, and they invariably joined the Peace Corps, the civil rights movement, or some other organization where the virtuous always find steady work. Pragmatism was valued much more highly than zeal. Priests are required to inspire blind faith in their flocks. They are required to impress upon their parishioners that, while God is all-loving, he demands rigid adherence to a long list of beliefs, that the penalty for transgression is not only dire but eternal, and that generous contributions to the church go a long way toward soothing God's more wrathful nature. Pragmatists go about the business of tending and shearing their flocks with the healthy knowledge that they are selling the only salvation available and that nothing, especially salvation, can be made available cheaply. After all, who would skimp on something so valuable as eternal salvation?

The saintly, over the centuries, kept stumbling over the misconception that salvation should be offered free by a militant church dedicated to spiritual riches and the treatment they received at the hands of their fellow clerics was always more vicious than any they received from atheists.

Suffice it to say that I was a pragmatist. I guarded my

heart as vigilantly as my genitals, the goal being not to allow either organ much exercise. And up until the wheel of fortune turned me upside down, I was less tempted by appeals to the heart than to sins of the flesh.

The dissertation that was my entrance into the bowels of the Vatican was, Monsignor Clanahan's criticism aside, a revolutionary bit of scholarship. Not that the ideas were novel. They had been around for centuries. But I applied them to a troublesome problem in a way that cast a historical pall over zealotry without raising doctrinal problems. The tract traced the cult of Mary back to a certain Sufi sect which had practiced the same kind of obsessive devotion. I traced the cult back through Saracen Spain, showing how it had been spread by troubadours and mendicants. I showed how it had been carried back in the saddlebags of returning crusaders and how it had gained momentum slowly until Mary threatened to transcend her rather humble role as Mother of God and become a goddess of equal rank with the *Trinity*. I shone the cold light of historical criticism on Mary worship without putting into jeopardy any rigidly defined dogma. I must say it was a brilliant piece of work.

Mary, you see, had become something of a problem. Beginning in the seventeenth century, just before modern warfare destroyed the postfeudal order of things, the Virgin began appearing to children, saintly young nuns, and Mexican Indian peasants, her message always simple and very pure. Pray, work for peace, turn away from militarism and materialism. Those she chose to visit were poor, uneducated, naive, rural innocents. To the horror of the Mexican hierarchy, she spoke in Indian dialect, not Castilian Spanish. Her apparitions, in vastly different parts of the world, were witnessed by people who had no way of knowing one another, yet she always appeared in remarkably the same form and garb. She left a shroud, healing wells, and a few unsettling prophecies in her wake.

While one might think that the Vatican would welcome, if not the universal message, then the publicity from these events, in reality, it shuddered every time word reached it of another apparition. The Church had not survived a few thousand years of wars, crusades, heresies, schisms, inquisitions, and revolutions just to let a few unscrubbed peasant children dictate to it "secrets" directly from Mary's lips. The Church Fathers had always seen to it that they had the final word and would have been infinitely more happy had the Virgin either appeared to *them* or stopped meddling in the Church's diplomatic affairs.

So they created a secret group whose duty it was to investigate these episodes without soiling the robes of the Vatican or letting legends build into mass movements that might leave the doctrinal niceties behind. At first this group was part of the Office of the Inquisition. When the more visible apparatus of the Inquisition was disbanded, the investigative branch was given its own offices.

CHAPTER TWO

Rome was everything to me. I was young, arrogant, and at every moment saw the unfolding of destiny. Rome was the brash Church, built one corrupt layer after another, grasping for temporal power and amassing incredible wealth in spite of a tradition and dogma steeped in poverty. And I loved her. Popes, even recent ones, were assassinated, poisoned, or drowned in the Tiber just to feed the insatiable beast of intrigue that substituted for more carnal obsessions. Rome demands the brazen show of sensuality or its most rigid purge. Had I only known then that the thing and its opposite are the same, it would have saved me nights of lonely writhing trying to shake off the *real* spirits that inhabit Rome.

I am, after all, a modern man. A man raised on the results of repeatable experiments. Vaccinated, made immune, by small doses of the poison of doubt so the result might be faith in the dual forces of authority and reason. Taught never to suspect the utter blindness of the one, nor to question the existence of the other.

Rome surged around me, a great impatient body of souls in search of enough; and should the goal of enough be reached, then excess. Wisely, they thought, the tonsured guardians tried to confine us to the Vatican, breaking us under the burden of scholarship. If Rome did not rest from its revels, neither did I from my studies. We studied the dangers that mystics, visionaries, and seers had always presented to the universal discipline Rome sought to impose. Beguines, Beghards,

Areopagites, Humiliates. Hadewijch of Antwerp, Hildegard of Bingen, Marguerite Porete, Hugh of St. Victor, Hildebert of Lavardin, Irene of Lyon, Marie d'Oignies, Mechtilde of Hackeborn. All had bathed in the love of a personal God and been sheltered from the gaze of history by a parched hierarchy who would deny to everyone the grace they sought in vain.

I dazzled my superiors with erudition. I traced songs of the ecstatics through the troubadours, through Islamic mendicants, through the emergence of courtly love poems, back further than Albert the Great, Duns Scotus, Benedict, Bonaventure, Denis, to the scholars and teachers of Baghdad, Constantinople, Alexandria, Damascus, Ephesus. I cut through their rude vernacular with the unwavering sword of research. My superiors whispered about me in the endless hallways where only the rustle of starched surplices and rumor are ever heard.

I had just turned thirty, but scholarship, blind obedience, and repressed impulses had already carved furrows in my cheeks. I looked like a bird of prey, kept hungry, wary, and mean like a falcon that must always surrender what it catches for a much more meager reward.

But the all too human songs of love the ecstatics had sung stirred me, reminded me of my manhood and spurred me to ever more obsessive bouts of study. My professors, had they been moderns with the slightest temptation toward psychology, might have seen the denial in my furious study, might have seen what was dammed behind what were only, after all, paper walls. They feared my devotion because it might prove devout. Instead they rewarded my ambition, which was one of the few emotions they sanctioned or understood.

The mystics and ecstatics wrote their visions, their love poems, and their songs of loss and anguish with one premise: that connection to God was direct, complete, and obliterated the self. They believed the self dropped away and became one with God through an emotional merger that was ecstatic. For the most part, they were silenced by the Inquisition, their writing unearthed only after the first stirrings of Vatican II. Suddenly their poetry reached across the centuries and was welcomed by groups of charismatics looking once more for mystic traditions outside the Latin aridity of orthodoxy.

Devotion to the Virgin cloaked the charismatic sects from the censure of Rome and gave them a link to the feminine aspects of Church doctrine in reaction to the paternalistic juggernaut of the hierarchy. Mary spoke directly in apparitions that seemed to cause symptoms of trancelike states in those who witnessed them. True charismatics, however, were not as interested in the apparitions that were witnessed by peasant children as they were in the fact that it was possible to have a direct emotional union with Mary.

Since my scholarship, which sheltered me from human contact, had been so incisive, I was chosen to investigate a modern beguinage in the Abruzzi hills east of Rome. A renegade priest, a few nuns out of habit, and a half dozen ex-cultists turned charismatics had taken over a deserted church and were scaring the local villagers with their rock-and-roll versions of the canonical hours.

Their leader, Father Dominic Poncarelli, had run across a Beguine manuscript while cleaning out a sacristy in Padua and was immediately struck by its relevance to the present. The Beguines shunned the strictures of Holy Orders and sought to be God, be one with God, through ecstatic experiences consisting of visions, time and space distortions, auditory hallucinations, and what can only be described as pseudo-orgasmic trances. The original Beguines had relied on courtly-love conventions for their inspiration, something that scandalized the hierarchies of the time, while their modern counterparts had whole worlds of Tantric, Buddhist, Reichian, and Gnostic philosophies to pick and choose among.

My superiors did not consider Poncarelli's group a

threat to anything except the general peace of the area, whose denizens consisted of hardheaded mountain people who relied on thousands of years of skepticism, xenophobia, and, more recently, Marxism, as charms against the decadence of dogma in any form.

They did not consider them a threat, that is, until the statue of Mary in Poncarelli's church began to weep on Friday afternoons. A few American tourists had heard vague rumors of the Weeping Virgin of the Abruzzi while waiting in line at the Vatican Museum. Soon busloads of tourists were grinding up the hills to the small town of Nerito before heading on to the ski slopes of the Grand Sasso. The people of the Abruzzi didn't care if the tourists spent money on their pilgrimage; they weren't going to carve replicas, build hotels, or in any other way ruin their peace of mind or surrender their dignity to hordes of Americans and Germans.

I arrived on a Wednesday in a freshly pressed cassock, carrying a hand-tooled Florentine briefcase filled with documents identifying me as a Vatican official. The documents gave me the necessary authority without clarifying exactly what that authority was.

It was spring in the mountains and the air was cold but cleaner than a Roman would think possible. Nerito had remained untouched by the passage of time, or at least time in the guise of *autostradas*, apartment complexes, universities, and factories.

In Italy, as in few other places, time is a palpable entity. In this village, all the buildings were made of stone and had been inhabited continuously for centuries. Many of the inhabitants were close to a century old themselves and, while their children and grandchildren moved in contemporary time, life for them remained essentially unchanged. Old women still walked the stone streets with bundles of kindling tied to their backs. Men still returned from the mountains with baskets of chestnuts and porcini. Sheep grazed on the small meadows tended by a single shepherd, who sat and stared at the unchanging mountains.

Father Poncarelli received me in the kitchen of a small house near the top of a narrow, twisting road. The room was just large enough for a table, a few chairs, a butane stove, and a tiny refrigerator. A faded reproduction of the Virgin was its only decoration. Poncarelli offered me espresso and we sat at the table and studied each other. He was stocky and almost bald. His face was contracted into a mask of seriousness, but it seemed an effort. Lines around the mouth and eyes hinted that his natural expression was laughter, and his whole body was tensed against a natural expansiveness. While he was serious, he was afraid neither of me nor my authority. And I was surprised to detect a glint of embarrassment in his eyes.

"I need not tell you that Rome views these reports of the Virgin weeping with the utmost seriousness," I began. "While it welcomes anything that promotes faith and devotion to Our Lady, still it must protect itself from deception and scandal." I was young and full of official zeal, which should never be mistaken for real zeal. I wanted to cast my inquiries in the harsh glare of official light, to impress upon him the weight of the authority vested in me. I shudder now to think of it. As though a few clerics isolated in their *palazzi* could decide what was real and invest a young fool with a little learning and vaulting ambition with enough authority to impose it.

"Believe me," he said, "I am the last one to want Rome's attention. In America I was hounded by my archbishop for opposing their wars and their treatment of refugees and farm workers. So I came here in peace, for peace, to do my work in isolation. I do not ask the Virgin to weep on my altar, but I do not question her wisdom in doing so. There is much for her to weep about. Still, still I tried to keep it quiet. To keep my peace and the peace of Rome. But it is not possible."

Poncarelli's star had been rising once too, but the wheel had taken a sickening turn when he began to protest the Vietnam War, thereby defying the authority of his bishop. If he had not had family in the Abruzzi and if he had not already had a small following, he would have joined the growing number of American clerics living outside Holy Orders. As it was, he lived a tenuous life, without official sanction, invisible to the hierarchy. He had reopened an abandoned church, fixed the roof and the altar with his own hands, and gathered a small flock from among his stubbornly agnostic countrymen. I believed what he said and believed the pained look in his eyes even more.

"And so you must agree that this incident must be treated with the utmost delicacy," I said. "I am here to investigate, and will report to my superiors a reasonable explanation that will leave the devotional aspects intact, while contradicting any suggestion of supernatural intervention." My coldness felt like a suit of armor. The threat was obvious. Father Poncarelli could not afford to be seen in an unfavorable light. There was no place to fall except from the wheel entirely.

"Your quarrel is not with me, Father D'Amato," he said slowly in an angry, defiant, yet defeated voice. "I will give you no trouble. You may have trouble narrowing reality to fit the version you require, and you may injure the delicate nature of faith and obscure the paradoxical path it often takes. You may even have reason to quarrel with yourself, but not with me." He stood abruptly, and with a studied ritual, washed the cups and put them away, cleaned the tiny espresso pot and put it away, and silently walked me to another small house where he had arranged for me to stay.

It was an old stone house with a spectacular view of the mountains over which loomed the Grand Sasso. A peasant's house. A place to live simply, at one with the surroundings. I understand now how one could find peace there. At that time, however, I felt confined, uncomfortable, insulted. I missed the constant reference points of gossip and intrigue the way a meteorologist might miss his barometer and altimeter. Poncarelli would pose no threat to Rome. His position was too precarious and he had no hope of improving it. I had not talked to the villagers or met his followers, but I knew from the dossier that Poncarelli had found them on the streets. They were runaways and former drug addicts. My goals were to find a plausible explanation, impress everyone with my authority, and wait for the attention of the pilgrims to waver.

That first night I sat by the fireplace and reviewed my notes. I found nothing to temper my optimism. Yet I felt uneasy, as though beneath the floor yawned the mouth of a chasm. I shook off the uneasiness, climbed the ladderlike stairs to a loft, and fell immediately into a dreamless sleep.

CHAPTER
THREE

I awoke early and watched the sun rise over the mountains. I felt rested and it made me uneasy. A scholar lives on stale coffee and exhaustion. In the tiny refrigerator I found eggs and prosciutto. I made coffee and drank it overlooking the village, which had been about its labors for hours. A few goats ran up and down the streets. Stonemasons were repairing a wall. Women were either tending their small gardens, pushing their scrubbed and impeccably dressed children off to school, or hanging their wash on the line. Behind them were heavily wooded hills dotted with tiny terraced gardens. Over all was the looming presence of the Grand Sasso eternally haloed by clouds.

After another cup of coffee, I walked, briefcase in hand, down to the church. The people I met nodded their respect but did not conceal their interest or their suspicion. The church had been built in the mid-sixteenth century. My notes said it had been burned twice, used as an Allied ammunition dump in World War II, and then abandoned until Poncarelli opened it.

Poncarelli, in old jeans and a T-shirt, with a red bandanna tied around his neck, was supervising the masons who were rebuilding the north wall of the church. Trowel in hand, he often joined in, expertly repositioning and setting a stone in mortar, all the while exhorting the workers. Among the middle-aged Abruzzi men were a few American youths who looked as if they had just awakened from a long restless sleep and found themselves in a foreign land with no clue of how to act or what to say. "Come on, get to work!" he would shout in Italian, then in English. "Paul, that mortar is too wet, more sand, man." Or "Sandro! Not that stone. The one behind you."

I watched for a few more minutes, then entered the church. It was rustic with only a few clerestory windows set high in the transept. Four huge beams supported the walls. Even in the intense morning light, it was dark except for a shaft of light that fell directly on the statue of the Virgin. I walked quietly toward the small alcove where the statue stood. It was in no way remarkable except that it was very old, sixteenth century probably, and carved from a single block of hardwood. I had studied innumerable statues of the Virgin, studied centuries of styles and the schools attached to certain places. This statue was primitive, although carved by a master. The Virgin appeared more as a startled young woman than as the Mother of God. She looked out on the world with shocked and troubled eyes as though she had seen too much of the sorry mess we had made of it. Her arms reached out from her body in a gesture of supplication. Her garments were painted an azure blue, her face the olive color of most Abruzzi women. I was moved by the simplicity of her plea. I walked slowly around the statue. Then I took out my pocketknife and carved a sliver of wood from the hem of her gown and slipped quietly out of the church.

I walked around the village, wandering past the line of houses into the hills along what must have been goat paths. I dozed in a small field, then returned in the afternoon and lunched on a hunk of salami and a piece of hard bread.

At about four I walked again down the path to Poncarelli's tiny rectory. He was waiting in the doorway, his stocky, powerful body almost filling the frame. He was back in clerical garb, a wrinkled cassock frayed at the hem and sleeves and Mexican sandals. He watched my approach and greeted me warmly, a half smile tugging at the corner of his mouth.

"The mountain air agrees with you, Gabriel. Perhaps Rome is bad for the health."

"Rome has more on her mind than my health, I'm afraid," I answered curtly.

"Of course."

We sat in a small, cluttered room at the back of the house. There were books scattered on the floor and blueprints tacked to the walls. A small desk lamp provided the only light. The room smelled of old books, cigars, and wet mortar.

"How long have you been rebuilding the north wall of the church?"

"A few months, perhaps three."

"The statue of the Virgin . . ."

"Beautiful, isn't she?"

"Was it here when you opened the church?"

Poncarelli hesitated. A strange expression of sadness spread slowly over his face. "A mystery, a complete mystery. She was not. When I arrived, the north wall was nearly gone. Many pews had been chopped up for kindling. The altar was found in a barn a mile away, the tabernacle in an old woman's house. She used it for a bird cage. Rats had eaten the candles and chewed on the candlesticks. Dust and rat shit covered everything. Fifty-millimeter shell casings littered the floor. Birds nested in the rafters. We opened the doors a year ago and they creaked violently, then the rusted hinges gave way and they shattered into splinters on the way down the stairs. Anything of value had long since disappeared. We cleaned and repaired and rebuilt. The townspeople kept their distance and watched us as though we were ghosts. One day an altar cloth appeared. I began to leave the doors unlocked at night. Nearly every day a candlestick, a small statue, or altar linen materialized, all in perfect condition, starched or polished or freshly painted. Food was left for us and wine.

"When I began to say Mass, no one from the village attended, except one old woman who mumbled the rosary loudly and then fell asleep and snored just as loudly. A few months later they began to trickle in on holy days. One Friday I opened up the church and next to the scaffolding on the north wall someone had erected a pedestal on which rested the statue of Mary and the floor in front of her was strewn with flowers. That is all I know."

"Her altar is now on the other side, the south side."

"Yes, of course. To rebuild the wall we had to move her. A few weeks later, on a Friday, I was saying Mass and I heard a gasp from the congregation. I turned and saw they were staring transfixed at the statue. What appeared to be tears had formed in the corners of her eyes. And her statue was illumined by a brilliant shaft of light from the window. Very dramatic. No one spoke of it afterward, but, as you might imagine, attendance at Friday Mass grew in geometric proportions. Soon the tour buses began to arrive, as well as papal investigators." He smiled at me sadly and looked out the small window next to his desk as though seeking a logical explanation in the mountains or the billows of clouds behind them.

"And do you have an explanation?"

"Explanations do not interest me. I am nearly dead of explanations, reasons, arguments. They are the smoke that obscures God. Here we do not pray *to* God, we do not ask his blessing on our wars and our banks, we try to be *with* God, to bathe in his mercy. And we recognize that the path leads through the conscious mind and out the other side."

"Father Poncarelli, if we are to avoid being reasonable, we should not also be impractical. Rome tries to honor its mystical past, but it must also avoid arousing the false expectations of the faithful. It may be important for you to delve into that mystical past, but that past was also fraught with many events of questionable veracity. I am here to investigate a phenomenon that occurred in a consecrated church under the jurisdiction of the Holy See. It is my responsibility to ensure that errors and misconceptions are not fostered in the name of Rome."

Poncarelli made a gesture of annoyance, stood up, and after a short search, returned with a bottle of scotch and two glasses. Without comment or invitation he poured until the glasses were full. "Father D'Amato, Gabriel, please, let us avoid preaching to one another. I love the Church as you do. I do not wish to fall into error or appear to create illusory phenomena. Nor do I wish to bore God with useless discussion. Talk of something else. Tomorrow, at any rate, is Friday and you will see for yourself. I am interested in your response, but not in your reasoned explanations. OK. Drink now and give me news of Rome and the world outside these mountains."

It was late when I left. The night air was cold and it was dark and I walked slowly up the hill, a hill that had, in a few hours, grown immeasurably steeper.

CHAPTER FOUR

The chanting that echoed through the village at Matins had an unearthly sweetness. I dressed quickly and hurried to the church. There was no light at any window and I passed no one on my way. I kept to the edge of the cobblestone streets and slipped silently through the side entrance of the nearly completed north face. A headache tugged at my temples. I was barely awake and unprepared for astonishment.

The altar was covered with wild roses and irises. It was lit by two candelabra that had not been there earlier. Poncarelli was in the center of the altar prostrate before a Baroque monstrance. He wore vestments of a modern design that looked East African. His followers, about twenty youths who ranged in age from eighteen to twenty-five and a few older women, were arranged in a semicircle around him. They knelt and sang. I recognized the prayer as one of Mechthild of Magdeburg's poems.

> The fish in the water cannot drown,
> The bird in the air cannot fall,
> Gold is not destroyed by fire,
> But there receives its shine and glow.
> God has given to all creatures
> The way to follow their own nature.
> How then could I resist my nature?
> I have therefore left all to enter into God
> Who is my Father by nature,

My brother by his humanity, my Betrothed by
   love,
And I am His since before time began.

I slipped into a pew in the back of the church where
light from the candles could not penetrate the darkness.
To my surprise Poncarelli's service had nothing to do
with the Virgin, had nothing to do with traditional
canonical hours. I was wondering what he was up to
when a young woman in a white tunic began to sway
back and forth. Soon the Beguine prayer ended and
they took up a chant, a long litany each versicle followed by the response *Ora pro nobis*. This might have
been more traditional but the rhythmic swaying, which
was now taken up by everyone, was not liturgical but
Brazilian. Poncarelli didn't move but provided each
versicle in a deep and passionate baritone that seemed
to set the rafters trembling syntonically. The response
was a blend of pure tenor and alto and I soon realized
I was breathing in unison, inhaling with the verse and
exhaling with the response. Before I realized what was
happening, I was caught up in the chant, my breath
deepening with each *Ora pro nobis*. My head cleared,
colors sharpened until each object and person was distinct in space. I almost began to sway but held myself
in check. I lost track of my thoughts, and images appeared, images from my past, not just recollections.
Events from my life seemed to be replayed in my imagination, events of troubling sensual impulses and
long-repressed sexual urges. I felt as though an electric
current were pulsing through my veins.
   The chanting was now broken with counterrhythms
which moved up and down the scale in impossible chro-
matic shifts. Poncarelli's verses lengthened and his voice
filled the church with reverberations that did not die
away before the responses embroidered the dying vi-
brations with their own ecstatic and bittersweet song.
   The girl who began the hypnotic swaying fell on her
side, her ecstasy replaced with a trancelike stillness.

One by one, each chanter fainted and lay still, until one woman was left to answer Poncarelli's voice. She was the oldest of his followers, a frail-looking woman of about fifty who answered the last of the litanies and then lay prostrate herself.

The silence left me almost unable to breathe. There were only the candles, which danced and hissed as they burned, and the endless reverberations of Poncarelli's bass. I found I could not move, never wanted to move again. I felt only a kind of surrender, a pleasant emptiness, the sensation of not needing to breathe again while I listened to my blood, shocked at first to think I was experiencing death. It was only much later that I realized it was love.

CHAPTER FIVE

When I awoke, it was morning, and I was curled up on a pew. Someone had put a rolled-up altar cloth under my head as a pillow. I sat up refreshed, a little disoriented, and very angry. My conscious mind searched what it knew about hypnotically induced experience resulting from rhythmic repetition and movement. I knew from studying Islamic texts that dancing and chanting could lead to trance states. I knew that the secrets of these experiences involved a mixture of sensory deprivation, controlled breathing, and incremental repetition until the conscious mind surrendered to the unconscious. It was one thing to read a monograph describing these states, it was quite another to be drawn into one myself.

I suddenly became aware that a shaft of light shone on the statue of the Virgin. She seemed to shimmer in the light. A few old women in black dresses knelt before her. Slowly the space around her altar filled with women. No one glanced in my direction. Their eyes were fixed on the statue as their mouths told their beads. A group of nuns arrived, filing silently up the side aisle until they joined the group that now formed a semicircle about four deep around the Virgin.

The shaft of light began to climb up the statue. The focus changed minute by minute. The light seemed to flow like a glowing liquid. By the time it reached her hands there were over a hundred people deep in prayer. A collective gasp of anticipation escaped as the light neared the Madonna's face. A nun began to lead the rosary in a loud authoritarian whisper and soon every-one was praying in unison. After the night before, this filled me with apprehension. I peered closely at the faces but none of them seemed to be part of Ponca-relli's band.

My gaze was drawn back to the statue. The sunlight was directly on her face now and she had acquired a halo of white light. I was moved again by her expres-sion, as though she were a young woman caught up in divine business beyond her comprehension, as though the cruel machinery of history could only deepen her compassion and tenderness. Then, to my astonishment and the cathartic cries of the devout, a tear hesitated at the corner of her eye, made a slow arc down her cheek, and fell into the open bloom of a wild rose. Many wept as they continued to pray, their prayer now more like a lamentation.

There I knelt, facing spirituality without direction, unwilling to see it become directed without spirit and just as unwilling, for my own reasons, to simply walk away from it. Of course I already had a hypothesis that fit a scientific model. That part of the equation posed no problem. What was problematic was the fact that I was being exposed to valid experiences of desire for spiritual union, all of them true and all of them in error.

One can certainly live in a world of Poncarelli's eclecticism and his charismatic desire to experience God. One can live in a world of weeping Madonnas where symbolic gestures and messages might pass di-rectly between the seen world and the unseen world. But one cannot manage a Church based entirely on charisma or mystically charged messages. *Upon this rock I will build my Church.* Someone must decide what is acceptable and what is in error. The Roman Catholic Church had always erred on the side of error. In other words, the hierarchy was always the repository of unchanging truth and always deferred to other long-dead hierarchies, making nearly all contemporary phenomena into error and leaving all long-held belief true. There are small windows of opportunity, but very few.

I knew the devotion of the people who witnessed the tears of the Virgin to be real. I knew the message received was received properly, but I had to debunk the reality of the medium. If the statue of the Madonna wept into the outstretched hands of a cardinal, my task would have been easier. Why that had never happened was a mystery that interested me. Perhaps their hands were too busy elsewhere. My path was clear, nevertheless. I had been trained not to be deluded by my feelings or the witness of my senses. From the clarity of my present meditations, from the promontory over the abyss I now peer into, I can see that the anger I experienced was directed toward myself. But it was Poncarelli and these devout pilgrims who were going to be the recipients of it.

I stalked out of the church, fired with the zeal of a rationalist. I saw everything. It took two rapid trips around the church before I understood what had happened. I had my explanation. I just couldn't explain the coldness in my heart that made me tremble as I returned to my rooms to pack.

CHAPTER
SIX

Had the coldness always been there? The first time I saw a priest I was taken by his kindness, the kindness engendered by the separateness of his existence. *To be in the world but not of it.* My earliest memories are of that separateness. Not superiority, that is just a dressing on the wound. But I felt I was marked for solitude, marked in a way that was visible to others but invisible to me. I made vain attempts at normalcy, all of them blocked by a painful self-consciousness, as though I could watch the interaction from outside myself and find myself wanting. Becoming a priest meant acknowledging that mark and using it to gain respect, using it as a way to move through the world without the expectation of joining it.

I entered the seminary at thirteen. My family and friends thought I was too young for such a decision, but I had the seriousness of one marked by destiny. The seminary was a place that specialized in making that invisible mark visible. It had a forbidding stone façade, with its dormitories forming a square with it. In the center was a courtyard around which rose an arched colonnade like a Spanish mission. Around the building stretched about a hundred acres of land, a baseball diamond, tennis courts, swimming pool, and a small stream shaded by oaks.

The day began with a Latin mass at 5:45. We were force-fed a diet of Latin and Greek classics: Caesar's *Commentaries*, Virgil's *Aenead*, Cicero's *Orations*, Sallust, Horace, Plato's *Apology*, as well as the Gospels. It was a circumscribed world ruled by silence and punctuated by bells that awakened us, got us to chapel, to meals, to class, and back to chapel. Meals were taken in silence before which was read the martyrology, the stark chronicle of who was burned at the stake, crucified, or roasted on a spit that day in Church history. We all had favorite martyrs the way other boys had favorite baseball stars.

There was beautiful St. Agnes, who was stripped naked before beginning a humiliating walk to the Colosseum. Her hair miraculously grew long enough to cover her. Or St. Polycarp who was roasted on a spit, whose last words were "I'm done on this side, turn me over." Or St. Peter himself who, about to be crucified, still smarting from his betrayal of Christ in the Garden of Gethsemane, demanded to be crucified upside down because he was not worthy to die in the same manner as the Lord.

Prostrate on the cool stones of the cathedral, scenes are repeated, moments frozen in the long pilgrimage to a frozen heart. There is a memory, an image of kneeling in prayer in my room, my arms outstretched, willing the special touch of God. The stigmata burned into the hands and feet of Francis; springs of healing waters gushed from the ground; signs appeared in the sky that augured battles; saints were blessed because they whipped themselves or lived in caves or starved, or were torn apart by horses, boiled, blinded, or barbecued. I found I could pray with my arms outstretched for about one minute. I longed for visions, for my priestly vocation to be acknowledged by the cosmos. But my meditations were notable only for their distractions.

We were, in truth, normal boys driven by family pressures, or abnormal boys driven by family pressures, or misfits who felt they had been called in order to give meaning to their role as societal outcasts. I had no talent for self-mortification and no visionary experiences, no saintly impulses, only a desire to excel intellectually, coupled with a passion to stand out as more alone than the most lonely.

I remember the warm autumn evenings, the darkening blue of the sky as we walked to a forbidden promontory well off the path that wound around the grounds of the seminary. We made a ritual of these evening walks. We always went to the same place, a hill overlooking the city that seemed to spread as we watched. The *world* started at those lights, the world of struggling masses of people whom we were bound by our vocations to save, yet just as fiercely taught to fear. We stood and talked. We understood the dilemma. As it grew darker, the lights of the city brightened, and we became young men, not only sheltered from the life of the senses, but also thrown into the depths of metaphysical questioning.

If anyone were to waver along the path to the priesthood, I guessed it would have been me. So many of my classmates seemed more suited to the life. But six years later, it was my forehead that was anointed. On that day I knew that the process of separateness was complete. I did not think of the world as souls I might save, but as a fathomless ocean from which I had been fortunate enough to be rescued alive.

If my meditation uses the wheel of fortune, my dreams take other directions. Every night for years I have found myself being dragged into the darkness by the horrible animals that inhabit the façades of the great cathedrals. Beasts created to ward off evil terrify me and visit upon me nightly vivid horrors as they drag my body across the stones. Lions with huge wings and the talons of immense eagles carry me by the neck over ground I invariably recognize. Great buzzards with the faces of ghouls fixed in expressions that warn of the unimaginable tortures of damnation carry me toward the abyss of their nests. The devils of the portals of Notre Dame and Chartres leer in triumph as they prod me along.

Before Freud and Jung rudely forced the locks on

the unconscious, the Church had a tradition of prophetic dreams and dream analysis. Old Testament, to be sure. But angels were always breaking into someone's dreams and giving them special instructions and messages, usually warnings about dire events that would occur should they not repent. Although modern psychology did not exist for the Church, still we were taught that dreams and visions were often the frequency God chose to broadcast his messages and orders. I did not have the faith necessary to believe that my dreams were being singled out for special divine attention, but I felt they must have a deeper meaning and they troubled me. I would awaken in the middle of the night covered with sweat and mortal foreboding. I associated these beasts with evil and with death. The darkness that moved ever closer was immense and without boundary. The more I tried to control my anxieties, the more intellectual, scholarly, and dogmatic I became.

One day not long ago, while saying Vespers alone in the Church of San Pietro in Montorio, on an afternoon when the sky had cleared after a rain, it came back to me. It was a memory of my first Easter as a seminarian. During Holy Week all the statues were covered with purple and all the bells silenced. Wooden devices that made a loud clacking noise were used to wake us up or send us to chapel.

Classes were suspended in midweek and there was time to read and meditate. Even the smell of freshly mown grass came back to me. On Good Friday we sang the Passion and were silent the rest of the day. The next day was spent conscious that the light that animated our spiritual lives had been killed. At dusk we were sent to our rooms and awakened just before midnight. Wearing cassock and surplice, we filled the courtyard. Candles were passed around to everyone. Then the rector lit a small pyre and the new light was passed from him to the senior professors and from them to the students until the darkened courtyard was ablaze. As I watched the light grow from one spark to a sea of light my heart swelled with emotion.

Carefully guarding our candles, we walked in silence into the chapel. When everyone was in his place, the choirmaster came forward and intoned the triumphant notes of the *Exultet*, whereupon the organ exploded in wild chords and the purple robes flew off the statues. It was then that I pledged myself to the priesthood and felt a kind of satisfaction that might have been happiness had not my dreams kept dragging me over and over the broken territory of my past.

CHAPTER
SEVEN

I left the Abruzzi defiantly. There were no salutations,
no final social exchange of pleasantries. I felt surrounded by the massive weight and power of the Vatican. It was a simple matter to entomb my emotions in
the great folds of stone drapery. On the train back to
Rome I began my report, underscoring again and again
with a fundamentalist's fervor the inherent dangers to
Rome in what Poncarelli and his band had created. The
age of saints, I said, could not be brought back in the
guise of mass hysteria. As for the weeping Madonna, it
was a simple phenomenon created by the rays of the
sun being reflected off the windows of Signora Savelli,
who only opened the shutters of her upstairs windows
on Fridays when she did her weekly cleaning.

What I found most disturbing was the possibility
that devout pilgrims would begin to soak up Poncarelli's
brand of direct religious experience. While Poncarelli
was harmless in himself, the kind of media attention
that would inevitably be focused on a movement that
had the Weeping Virgin of the Abruzzi as its symbolic
leader could do enormous damage to an already frac-
tious situation. So I recommended that the church be
brought under the direct supervision of the local
bishop, that Poncarelli be offered an even more remote
church, and that the statue be moved to a "more ap-
propriate and devout" setting, as far away as possible
from the supernatural influences of direct sunlight.

The statue itself was something of a mystery. I
guessed by its style that it originated in North Africa. I

had the sliver from the statue analyzed, and it came from a tree whose sap liquefied only when heated by intense and direct sunlight. The mystery was its arrival in the Abruzzi. But I reasoned that it could have appeared there in any number of ways. Relics and artifacts moved more freely than one might imagine. The looting of shrines had been the favorite pastime of soldiers in every war. In fact, war had always been the most efficient distribution method for ideas, national treasures, and social diseases. Italians had spent a dozen years unsuccessfully resuscitating the Roman Empire in Ethiopia and Libya, and I was certain a few boatloads of booty made their way back home along with the bodies of the fallen.

My report disappeared into the maw of St. Peter's and I heard nothing for a long time. It was late spring and Rome was washed by periodic rains that seemed to renew it. I moved out of the Vatican to a tiny apartment on the ascent to the Gianicolo that offered ever more spectacular vistas and ever more access to the narrow streets of the *centro storico* that had become my nocturnal haunts. I walked ceaselessly to avoid the nightly visitations that became infinitely more horrific as my control over already strangled emotions increased. Nights grew warmer and I added my heavy tread to that of the revelers with whom I shared my vigils. Down the Gianicolo into Trastevere and across the Ponte Sisto, through the darkened streets to the Campo dei Fiori. From the Campo across Vittorio Emanuele to the Piazza Navona where I wandered among tourists and pickpockets. I stood and watched the pomaded fortunetellers intent over their tarot decks, the wands and cups opening their tiny windows into the future. From the Piazza to the Pantheon where I sat and meditated over a sambuca, staring with endless fascination at the giant eternal message left by Hadrian to disguise his handiwork. M AGRIPPA F LUCIUS TER CON FECIT. From the Pantheon back to the Navona and then down the torchlit streets of the Via Coronari to the Via Giulia. Next I stood over the onrushing of the Tiber, the dome of St. Peter's at a safe distance, but farther than the inevitable nightmare that waited for me at the top of the stone steps littered with discarded syringes and condoms. I had outlasted the most hardy Roman. I had put off rest until dawn glowed over the eastern hills, until I had tired the beasts like a relentless matador.

Finally, I was summoned to Monsignor Signorelli's office. I waited in the outer office admiring his tapestries for only half an hour before an officious priest admitted me into his presence. Signorelli's bald head gleamed at me as it remained bowed over some documents. He didn't look up until I was seated and his secretary had retreated. His collection of medieval books was rumored to be the best in the world, as was his erudition and malevolence. His face was hairless, his eyes stuck in his head like two olives in a mass of kneaded dough. He was huge and his every movement had a monumental quality, as though it were being controlled from very far away. No one could remember a time when he wasn't there, no one had ever seen him outside of his office, no one had ever claimed to be his friend, to have eaten a meal with him, or seen him outside the Vatican walls.

"Father D'Amato, you have done well. Father Poncarelli is now the parish priest in a small town in Calabria. The name escapes me at the moment. A young priest, a native of the Abruzzi, has taken his place. A very strict young man, very serious. Most of Poncarelli's followers, if such is the term, have scattered, and the statue of the Virgin, newly ensconced in a small alcove, has ceased weeping. The tour buses have found other stops. Life in the village has returned to normal or whatever life in a village returns to after such events." He looked up at me then, although his eyes betrayed no emotion. "I trust you are rested for we have another assignment that involves a bit of travel. There is a church in England, in what they call the Midlands, I think. It is not a thriving parish, but it owns a few hectares of land in the vicinity and . . . there is something strange happening. It has been going on for a few years, but this is the first time it has affected Church property. The trouble is that it is not, per se, a religious phenomenon. You see, in the morning, the grasses or grains, or what have you, have woven themselves into complex, suggestive, and peculiar patterns. Most of them are large perfect circles. So large that, to get the proper perspective, one needs a helicopter. The grain lies in a clockwise whorl and is not damaged or broken, which is very odd indeed. No one sees or hears anything strange in the night. In the morning they are just there in the middle of a perfectly ordinary field.

"The Vatican desires that you investigate very, very discreetly. We want neither the notoriety of the Church's interest nor of its disinterest, understand? We expect, however, to learn enough so that, in the future, we will be able to make authoritative statements without making fools of ourselves. We would naturally prefer that these circles not appear on Church property, or be linked in any way with mystical Catholicism." He smiled a particularly wicked smile. "Unfortunately, we can no longer burn witches at the stake or rack them until they confess. Our options are so limited in the modern world. So we must be eternally vigilant. Any questions? You have been provided with papers that identify you as a priest who has been given leave to work through some ah . . . personal problems. Subtlety, Father, subtlety and discretion. Take long walks in the English countryside. It is not Tuscany, I can assure you, but . . ."

"How long will this investigation take?" I asked. I was disappointed. I had never heard of these crop circles and could see no way they had any relevance to Rome or to my career.

"A few weeks, perhaps a month." He caught my look of irritation and his eyes turned to stone. "We till the fields of the Lord, wherever they may be, yes?

"*Buon giorno*, Father, and by the way, this has been wandering about the Vatican." He handed me an envelope. "It is addressed to you. And one last thing. At some point we will wish you to stop in London for a few days and see Sir Henry Throckmorton. A very important contact, if somewhat difficult." Then he dismissed me with an imperial wave of the hand.

I walked back to my rooms through the arched gate, and along the Lungotevere. It threatened rain but I was too dejected to care. Great harbinger clouds divined and augured over me. Omens appeared in the shadows. The first drops fell as I began to climb the Gianicolo. I was soaked before I reached my cell-like rooms. I changed into dry slacks and shirt and sat at the window savoring, once more, through the fever of depression, the rooftops of Rome as the storm swept over, drenching them with long striations of rain. I brewed an espresso and returned to the window. The coffee had a biblical bitterness to it, like a cup of sorrows offered, accepted, and drunk to the dregs.

If anyone or any force cared to waste its time making circles in the grain fields of England, it was no concern of mine. But it was humiliating to impersonate a profligate priest, humilating and terrifying. It brought the beast of my dreams one step closer. Just when the most powerful clerics in the Vatican had begun to nod as I passed them in passageways, just when they had begun to listen to my requests, just when fruit and vegetable sellers in the markets had begun to greet me with salutations of respect and friendship, I must suffer the pitying glances, the downcast eyes, and the insolence of gossips. For I was sure that it was only status and respect that could keep nightmarish beasts at bay. Lately, they dragged me through scenes from my childhood, scenes of humiliation, shame, and sensual torment.

I grew up in a time and a place where, for some reason, the effects of Catholicism were particularly virulent. The American Church suffered the worst hangover from the Counter-Reformation. Gone was the Church of Christian forgiveness, charity, and instant redemption. And it would be years before anyone said that God was love.

In my meditations, Sister Mary Anthony loomed over me, the pale white flesh of her face made impossibly stern by the starched frame of her wimple. The days of fifth grade were the eternally hot afternoons of September. Endlessly we endured her lectures on sin. Sin was dirt and filth contrasted with the blinding white of her habit. Sin was the incessant pounding of nails into the sacred flesh of Christ. Her huge form eclipsed the light. She made us feel our every transgression was worthy of a bead of bloody sweat on Christ's brow.

Did I take it all seriously? For a long time, sin did not even connote sensual involvement. It meant small lies, disobedience, obscene jokes, swearing—not to speak of the sins of omission, the good I dodged or refused to do. It is not the concept of sin that was important to me as much as the fertile bed it provided in which inhibitions could take root.

For the children of that time, there was no one to temper the severity of the nuns with worldly pragmatism, with the idea that a loving God was more interested in our spiritual well-being than in the catalogue of our transgressions. No one preached that weakness of the flesh was natural, or that obsession with guilt could lead to dangerous neuroses. Cleanliness was next to Godliness and it was also close to the suburbs, close to the collection box.

Sin was everywhere. Yet some indomitable force in our personalities refused to bow to the constant tirades. Some force in our personalities, the green sap of youth, became the antidote to the spiritual madness. An antidote which, however, did not protect completely. Whereas I was always a rationalist intellectually, I succumbed to the Church's view of morality on the surface. I was not a hypocrite. I had no hidden vices then.

The inhibitions ran too deep for that. But I acted out of a rigid façade of goodness and virtue that had no grounding in deep faith. I expected my reward to be reflected in honors and respect. And of course the priesthood was the only career where that stance was still possible, the only career which sufficiently rewarded the bloodless results.

CHAPTER EIGHT

The rain stopped and I went to dinner at a small restaurant across the Tiber that offered fresh pasta and seclusion. Only then did I take out the letter Monsignor Signorelli had given me earlier. I looked it over carefully, then slit the end with my dinner knife and read the contents.

Dear Gabriel,

You are unaware of the favor you have done me, but let us call it a blessing in disguise. Since these are the only blessings that come my way of late, I won't complain. I am now the official pastor in a small town in Calabria. Sunburnt fields, goats, and an unfamiliar dialect. But I am very happy. No weeping Virgins, no band of followers to distract me from my meditations. I take long walks and I am on a first-name basis with most of the goats.

Although we spent only a short time together and had our differences, I feel somehow the kinship of brotherhood with you. We are not, after all, the sum total of our lives. There is something else living in us that is hidden from the daily transactions. You now make the choices that are demanded of your station. But do not be deluded by such appearances.

I am afraid you have become addicted to the seen, to the rationalized surface, while underneath exists another reality. It is this I respond to in you. For your own good, you must investigate the unseen, the intuitive, the lost abilities of Francis and Catherine—yes, even of Savonarola, not to mention mystics and visionaries and psychics outside our faith. There is in you an unacknowledged power and talent that has been strangled by your damned rationalism. Listen to your dreams. Make your dreams listen to you. You will suffer much at the hands of reason and to no purpose. But when the coat is worn through, you will realize you are warmer without it.

Poncarelli

I poured myself a glass of wine from the carafe and drank it slowly. I folded the letter, put it back in its envelope, and put the envelope in my inside pocket. I drank the dry white wine until the carafe was empty. The black bellies of clouds migrated overhead. I paid the bill and left.

I crossed the bridge and walked past the entrance to the Porta Portese market. It was deserted except for small cyclones of discarded handbills. I wandered the streets of Trastevere, letting the chill night air envelop me. It was about ten o'clock but the streets were just beginning to fill up with couples going to dinner and their offspring on Vespas searching for a party. I climbed the hill quietly so as not to disturb the lovers or the addicts. I stood at the top of the hill by the Fontana Paola and stared out at Rome. I was looking at the most beautiful and moving cityscape in the world. I could not understand why tears streamed down my cheeks to ruin the starched perfection of my collar.

On the ride to Fiumicino I read the hastily collected literature on crop circles, Druids, and English mysticism. There was little to hold my interest in any of it. Madame Blavatsky seemed to have done a good business for a while with her Theosophists. Gurdjieff had camped in England when he needed rich patrons. All easily dismissed as British eccentricity. The Druids, from the little information I was given, were a savage bunch who cavorted in sacred oak groves and promoted each other as candidates for human sacrifice. Their philosophy neatly avoided the duality that underpins Christianity. There was no good and evil, the light did not have the benefit of Genesis in being separated from darkness. There was a deep sense of power and mystery invested in rocks and trees and certain plants and in a kind of Celtic shamanism that manipulated it. Of course, except for a few eccentrics that Blavatsky and Gurdjieff missed, there is no real Druidism left.

The choices seemed to be either to retreat into a Druidic primitivism where the rocks and trees and the earth itself was alive and trying to communicate a message, or to believe some alien spacecraft was using the English countryside for maneuvers or target practice. My superiors favored neither explanation. The circles were abstract up to a point, neither overtly pagan nor Christian. But they were done with a disturbing precision, the grain bent flat without breaking the stems, as though the result of downward blasts. Yet stalks outside the circle were not even touched. Sometimes there was a circle with a perfectly concentric circle around it. Or a series of circles that looked like a die from the air.

The plane landed at Heathrow in the middle of a thunderstorm. Everyone clung to their faith and cinched their seat belts very tight. I collected my bags and took a bus to Victoria Station.

It was noon and Victoria Station was chaos on earth. I stared at the departures board, finally making sense of its hieroglyphics. After standing in an endless but, by Roman standards, well-behaved line, I purchased a ticket, found the platform, took my seat, and settled in for the three-hour trip. It was then I decided to confront my new persona.

I was to be Father Wolfe, an American professor of history at the Holy Names College in California. My personal problems stemmed from teaching and preaching liberation theology. While not exactly at that moment heretical or condemned, still it came too close to Catholicism's making amends with Marxism. It taught that the poor had a God-given right to struggle for social justice, even if it meant the overthrow of the present order. Some clerics saw this as permission to join armed insurgencies against juntas and regimes that enjoyed warm relations with the Vatican. A program was begun to silence the liberation theologians, to send them away for periods of "reflection and meditation." So, as Father Wolfe, I was not to preach, but to say Mass and mix as little as possible with the parishioners.

The train finally began to pull away from the platform and I looked up and smiled. At least I wasn't a hopeless drunk, a child molester, or an embezzler! Heresy I could handle. I rested my head against the plush headrest and watched the blighted industrial slums slowly blend into bleak suburb and finally into the classic British countryside, some of which recalled Wordsworth, or even more, Lawrence and sometimes Dickens. I glanced around the cabin. There was a young, very beautiful black woman who wore black tights, a man's white shirt, and a length of thin industrial chain as a belt. Her long shining black hair was pulled back and over it she wore a bowler. She glanced at me once or twice and then got absorbed in one of those strange British tabloids that tracked the sexual exploits of the Royals interspersed with tales of two-headed Pekingese and photos of barebreasted women. The only other person making the journey was a sixty-ish matron, all tweed, flowered hat, and sensible shoes. She was equally engrossed in reading the same newspaper. The rain had settled in and the countryside disappeared except as an even grayness punctuated with flashes of far-off lightning.

A liberationist? I relaxed and dozed and awoke with the young woman over me, saying, "Padre, hey, Padre, isn't this your stop?" I looked up at her and it took a moment to remember who I was, or at least who I was supposed to be.

"Yes. I see. Thank you."

My voice sounded like the voice of someone else, far away and awkward.

"I heard you ask the conductor. This is it, isn't it? Well, come on then."

I got my bag and briefcase and followed her from the train. Although I am a fast walker, I had trouble keeping up with her. She had a determined and confident gait. It was raining steadily and, once outside the shelter of the station, she popped open her umbrella with one hand and flagged a taxi with the other. A taxi skidded to a halt and we jumped in, instant coconspirators.

She held out her hand. "Jenny. Glad to meet you, Padre, but, I mean, you almost woke up in bloody Scotland. Where are you staying? I'm at a pension just down the street from St. Jerold's." She laughed easily and her voice was like music.

"I am staying for a while at St. Jerold's, ah, assisting the pastor." I smiled weakly and shook her hand. "I'm Gabriel."

"Really? I didn't pick you for R.C. Oh, well, old Jerold's could use some assisting. I mean drafty, rundown, and backward. I hear even the steeple leans to the right. I'm here doing some research. Call them crop circles here. Anthro post-doc work. Only interesting thing for miles and miles unless you're hung up on dry toast, warm beer, and skinny soccer players. You want to go looking, give me a call. Might not interest a Padre, but if you ask me, they are strange, as in strange." She wrote her phone number on the back of a matchbook, sat back and lit a Player's with one fluid motion.

I looked at her for a moment and returned her smile. "Since it's the only game in town, yes, I would enjoy it very much."

The taxi stopped in front of St. Jerold's. "You get tired of assisting, you just ring me up, hear?" I got out into the rain, took my bags, paid the driver the whole fare over Jenny's protestations, and walked up the short flagstone path to the rectory.

Jenny was right. The church was a dreary Gothic that had barely survived a few attempts at restoration. It looked as if each attempt had been halted for a century or so until new funds or energy could be found to begin again. The rectory, however, was more recent by a few hundred years, unimposing and unassuming brick flanked by a rose garden that would probably be beautiful in the summer. I didn't intend to stay long enough to find out.

I knocked forcefully on the front door, which was opened immediately. I dodged in out of the rain and was greeted, if that is the word, by Father Brian Dunstan. "Ah, Father Wolfe, I see you've found us." He was just short of monolithic, about six-four, close to three hundred pounds, unruly hair, a pockmarked face and eyes cut from a piece of inferior slate. He did not smile, which made his greeting more an accusation. I was sure a smile would have done irreparable damage to his face.

I looked around. To one side of the entry was a comfortable enough room, meaning it had a gas fire and what looked to be a well-stocked bar. On the other side was a formal dining room with a huge table and high-backed chairs. Straight ahead was the stairway leading to the second floor.

"Upstairs. First door to the right. Dinner at eight sharp, drinks, if you want, half past seven." I nodded and walked toward the stairs, stopping a second for a closer look at the living room. It appeared no one had opened the heavy green drapes in years. There was an old couch and a few uncomfortable-looking chairs. It was musty and smelled of stale cigars. I kept walking up the stairs and into a dark hallway. I groped for the door to my room.

The room I entered was a surprise. It had been freshly painted. There was a vase of flowers on an antique chest of drawers. In the center of the room was a bed with a goose-down coverlet. The drapes were open, revealing a mullioned window that offered a view of the church and the surrounding countryside. I unpacked my few clothes and books and then stood at the window for a long time.

CHAPTER
NINE

I came down to dinner resolved not to be surprised or intimidated. Dunstan was waiting for me. He was standing in front of the fire, his legs apart, his arms folded behind his back. When he saw me, he moved to the bar and looked down at me and mixed two drinks from a crystal decanter. "Whiskey's all right, I hope," he said, handing me a water glass half full.

"Quite," I shot back, trying to seem British. He raised one eyebrow slightly as I tasted it. It was splendid. He nodded slightly and sipped his.

"Old friend of mine is pastor of a church in the north of Scotland where the North Sea is fierce and the people are as hard as the land, but the whiskey is a plenary indulgence." I sipped in agreement. "It is not much better here, mind you. There is a longer growing season, yes, but the hearts are just as hard. We have a handful to work with, but it barely supports one, and him meagerly. I am a strain on the diocese, but they don't dare close St. Jerold's. The Church owns land in the area, has for centuries, and while we hardly see a nickel from it, it helps to have the church open. Besides, there's no place to send me. This is the end of the line." He raised his glass and drained the contents. "Dinner," he said with a small bow, "is served."

I looked around, then back at Dunstan. He looked at me for a moment, went into the kitchen, and came back with a tray on which were two plates, some smaller bowls filled with odd-looking sauces, and two bottles of dark beer. "Sit down, Father, sit down. You think there is money here for a housekeeper, you think this is St. Paul's? The only flocks here are real sheep and even they are not well fed. And the shepherds are a bunch of brooding pagans.

"I spent a bad war before I was a priest. Gunnery sergeant in Burma, protecting the lads who were cutting the Burma road. Nasty business. But I learned a bit about surviving in hostile territory, and I learned about prayer, most of it praying over the dead."

"Is this hostile territory?"

"Not completely, Gabriel, not completely. It's like that Old Testament story about the widow and her son who go to the larder every day and there is just enough to get by, never too much, never nothing." He ate in silence for a while and looked at me as though he just remembered I was still there. "The bishop's secretary said nothing about why you are here. But if they sent you here, you know, it was not a promotion."

I took a few gulps of beer. "My superiors decided I needed a rest."

"You look fit enough to me."

"A rest somewhere out of the way, where there was a church but not much preaching required."

"They've clapped a hand over your mouth, then?" he thundered. "Were you preaching the Albigensian business, what?" His face clouded with anger, but I wasn't sure of its direction. I forged ahead.

"Not heresy, no, not heresy at all, but social justice, Father Dunstan, the notion that the Church must be involved in social change."

"Good God, they've sent me a bloody firebrand," he roared.

I looked at him with alarm. "A silenced one, I'm afraid."

"The swine."

"Swine?"

"Look at them, look around here. Church empty except for a few old dodderers who wouldn't know a dogma from a dog license. The rich go High Church for the status, the poor, some blithering fundamentalist or other. Silenced, you say? And for saying the Church must be in the vanguard? Fight for souls and for food so they don't starve, and clothes so they don't go naked. Silenced? Never heard of such a thing."

"Haven't you been following the controversy over liberation theology?"

"Behind on me controversies, I guess. Haven't gotten past them burning poor Savonarola or Giordano Bruno."

"You *are* behind. Giordano Bruno?"

"Hobby of mine, poor bloody Bruno." We had finished dinner by then. "Come here," he said, and led me into the front room. He stood in front of a shelf where there was arranged what looked to be a complete library of Giordano Bruno's writings. There were also French and British histories of the period and a thick portfolio of papers. As I gazed, a fusillade of questions forming in my mind, Dunstan went over to the bar and poured two glasses of sherry. "Celebration is in order, actually."

"What is there to celebrate?"

"The conclusion of my detective work."

I looked at him. There was a strange gleam in his eyes that made him look only slightly less ugly. He had the solitary nobility of one who has carved out his place and wishes for no other. With shock I realized I had never seen that look before.

"Drink up, Father. Since you've been silenced, it's up to me to do the talking.

"Some time ago, years, when I first realized this was my last stop, and why, and what this posting meant, I thought I would go mad. Priests go mad, or they leave, or they take to the bottle. The sin of drunkenness, eh, Father? Mostly the bottle, and I was tempted. Even began to say Mass with port. Oh, I was headed down the long road all right. I walked, I gardened, I read. Odd thing was, I didn't pray much. Seems I used to pray when I was afraid of death, or wanted something to go my way. I was so bloody bored up here I was looking for death, and couldn't think of a thing I wanted. Nearly lost my faith. Then I ran across the story somewhere of how they burned Giordano Bruno for heresy. And I thought, if I could understand the heresy and work backward, I could understand faith, and I might get mine back. Quite mad, really.

"Opposite almost happened. The swine burned him for damned little and none of it heretical."

"They burned him in the Campo dei Fiori in Rome."

"Quite, and they made a show of it too. So I started to read backward and forward. I learned he was in England for a few years. Seemed odd. Bruno was working as the chaplain for the French ambassador at the court of Queen Elizabeth. Imagine him, Bruno, born in Nola, near Naples, finding himself in the same town as Sidney, Raleigh, Drake, Shakespeare, and the rest. Imagine him, one of the best minds of Europe, an errand boy for the fat Frenchman." He reached over and filled our glasses again.

"The nights are long here, Father, I can assure you. No telly. Not many friends. Well, I started to read the surrounding history, French and Italian and English. Porridge. Most of it porridge. Boring you yet, Gabriel?"

"Fascinating," I said. "Please go on."

"As you know, of course, there were no nations as we think of them. Duke of this or that. Kings, or in this case, queens, had the devil's own time raising money for wars and such. And the English were always at the throats of the French, and France was mucking about in Italy, and the Italians were all at war with one another, right? Remember also, don't you, that the pope was that madman, Paul IV, who excommunicated Elizabeth and tried to foment a revolution against her. Ended up destroying the Church in England once and for all. He made traitors of us all. The bloody pope thought he owned England and the monarchy just rented it from him.

"But diplomacy is still diplomacy. So you have our

fine young Bruno attached to the French ambassador. Intrigue. He was already a defrocked Dominican by that time. He had wandered about Europe teaching some strange system of memory at the University of Paris. And his work came to the attention of Henry III. Oh, he was versed in all the new learning: Copernicus, Ficino, Cornelius Agrippa, Lull. Questioned everything.

"You know, Luther was already launched, the Inquisition was burning witches and sowing chaos everywhere, and the Council of Trent had already tried to stuff the goose feathers back into the pillow.

"I haunt the old booksellers in London, and the British Museum, naturally, when I can get away. Middle of the week, if no one dies suddenly, away after Mass and back for dinner. Who's to miss me? 'An old man is a useless thing.' Anyway. I found this old book of letters to Elizabeth. From a Monsieur Fagot. Written in a quite intriguing code. Took me the best part of five months to crack it. Roses nearly died. But Monsieur Fagot, a pseudonym, of course, was passing information to the queen about certain plans the French had. Fagot was, in short, a spy.

"There was very nearly a parish revolt, as if they were up for it. I would show up late for Mass, in rumpled cassocks, lights on all night running up the electric bill. They thought I was having one on. The good ladies of the Altar Society smelled my breath, waiting for me to stumble, lose my place in the Gospel. I was at my wits' end. Who the bloody hell was Fagot? The name is a pun on both the English and French word for the bundles of branches they lay at your feet before they burn you. Macabre sense of humor, or prophetic. Another?" He filled our glasses again. The rain beat rhythmically on the slate roof. I did not know how much time had passed. I fought the effects of the sherry and redoubled my efforts to listen.

"All this time, mind you, the intellectuals, who suddenly weren't just clerics anymore, and even if they were clerics were worldly, urbane, after all . . . The intellectuals were meeting, sharing documents, bits of learning. And our boy Bruno was one of the youngest and the smartest, with the sharpest tongue and no love lost for the madman pope and his bloody retinue. Ah, he was beautiful and loved to talk and talked too damn much. Made enemies, I'm afraid." I thought he was going to crush his glass. He tossed the sherry back. His face contorted with emotion. He was fighting a five-hundred-year-old war.

"Word got back to Rome. Remember, it was a hey-day for the Inquisition, Cardinal Bellarmine chopping his way through the new thinkers and alchemists. What Bruno thought he was doing escapes me. But he continued to write and think and act too boldly. And the letters of Monsieur Fagot kept appearing before the monarch, Elizabeth the Queen. And he warned her of a plot to assassinate her, which caused a few prominent heads to roll. Now there were two bloody plans cooking between Rome and Paris. In one scenario, there was a plot to marry Elizabeth to the duc d'Anjou, which would have made a mighty alliance. But it would also mean there would be a king, a king who was Catholic, who would surely, surely return England to the fold. Our good Elizabeth, still smarting from being excommunicated and anathematized, would have none of him. So the next plot, involving her physician and a prominent duke, was to poison her. It was this plot, which of course was percolating about in the French Embassy, that Fagot uncovered and about which he warned Elizabeth. Bruno also loved Elizabeth and hated Rome and all it then stood for: corruption, simony, excesses of power, madness, and brutality. When Paul IV died, Rome rejoiced for days and would have thrown his body in the Tiber if the curia hadn't buried him quickly and deep.

"Bruno next showed up in France, then Germany, where he was too close to the Lutherans. Some say he was part of a plot to raise a German army and rid Rome of the popes forever. Finally, he was lured back to Italy with the promise of a position and arrested on a charge of heresy. Interrogated for a few years. After a few years, they shipped him to Rome in chains. In Rome his friends abandoned him, he was thrown in the Castel Sant'Angelo and put on trial for seven years. Seven years, mind you, in the Castel Sant'Angelo is no Roman holiday. Then one day he was carted over to this damned Campo of yours and the fagots, I can tell you, were put to his feet. Stripped naked, a wooden wedge stuck in his mouth. The fire was lit and he burned to death.

"Now what do you think? Case closed. The smell of burning flesh was remembered for a long time. If it weren't for his friends in London, most of his writing would be lost too. But one day I woke in the morning and there it was. Monsieur Fagot's letters stopped when Bruno left England. As soon as I could, I went to the British and looked at the manuscripts again. Bruno's and Monsieur Fagot's. Not conclusive, understand, but take it all together and Giordano Bruno was a spy for *Her Majesty*. The name Fagot, his dislike for Roman authority, the letters stopping when Bruno leaves England. By God he *was*, I just know it."

He stopped. I knew he was telling me because I too was an intellectual outcast washed up on the shores of England by what he must have divined as providence. What he did not know was that I was a spy, and that secret almost made me choke on the last sip of sherry. What he did not know was that I was a spy for the same papacy at whose whims both he and Giordano Bruno had suffered.

"Father Dunstan, it is an amazing story. What will you do with the information?"

He just stared at me. "No. You see it was like looking at the wrong side of the glass. I couldn't get back to my faith from heresy that wasn't heresy, but a man caught out of his time. They finally found a few records of his trial by the Inquisition, a kind of digest. They asked him why he thinks there are innumerable stars and planets, when the Church taught that the earth was the center of a small and lonely universe. And he answers that the nature of God is infinite and what could better glorify his infinity but infinite works. Beautiful, what? Find an answer to that. And what of the Virgin Birth, queries that fox Bellarmine. Our Bruno states flatly it's impossible. Ah, but didn't that pop the buttons on their cassocks, didn't they think they had him? But Bruno goes on. It's impossible for a virgin to give birth in the way we know, but since God chose miraculous methods of conception, perhaps he chose miraculous methods of delivery. Can't you just see the sweat appear on the upper lips of those curial jackals? It goes on, Gabriel, like this on and off for seven years. A lot of the time Bruno was too sick or weak to stand, but he was always ready with an answer. He was no real heretic. And this was bloody 1600, long after Columbus, and my God, Galileo was already peering into his telescope and getting himself in trouble. But they burned him anyway. Burned him anyway." He looked tired and older suddenly. "It is late, Father. Thank you for listening to an old man."

"Good night, Father."

He shook his head. "Silenced," he said.

I closed the door to my room gently. I stared at my image in the mirror for a few minutes. How could I go on with this charade? I tried to read but the words meant nothing to me. I paced, stood at the window, then paced some more. The sherry finally wore me down and I fell into bed, a priest on his way to developing personal problems.

CHAPTER TEN

The next day was clear and the sun was somehow out of place with the landscape. I had prepared myself for British gloom and would have been a little more comfortable had just one of my prejudgments proved true. I awakened early, about six, dressed and went down. I found some coffee and brewed it, but it was nearly undrinkable. I walked over to the sacristy and assisted Dunstan at Mass. We had agreed to trade off during the week and I needed to know how to open up, where the vestments were kept, how the lights worked, and how to open the safe which kept the wine and the supply of hosts. The ritual of the Mass had always had a calming effect. It made no difference that there were only six parishioners, none of whom came forward to take communion.

If my superiors had chosen this place as one of exile, it would have been perfect. Had I the fire of the teacher and the reformer, I would have found it the perfect torture. Although I had no such need, still the loneliness sent chills down a spine created by loneliness.

Dunstan and I cleaned up and locked the church. It did not wear even its Gothic mantle with enough style to draw tourists or architecture students. We made breakfast together and found little difficulty working in close proximity. Dunstan dug out some wonderful Indian black tea that almost made me forget coffee.

He found an old bicycle and I spent the morning wandering around the town shopping for dinner and allowing myself to be watched for suspicious tendencies.

I rode back to the rectory and found a note from Dunstan saying that he would be gone for the day and would return for dinner. So I wandered about the rectory, looking at the books in his small library, snooping in the cupboards and sideboards. I found nothing of interest except an extensive collection of opera recordings and a complete set of D. H. Lawrence. I found no evidence that he had investigated crop circles. I found no evidence that he had investigated anything past the sixteenth century. I went to the kitchen and made a tomato sauce for dinner. I left it to simmer and went upstairs to study the crop circle material again. I found everything except the information I needed, the precise locations of the circles that intersected Church property. I went back downstairs and searched until I found a survey conducted many years before. It showed St. Jerold's holdings with all the parcel boundaries. I had narrowed the variables considerably, but I still had no idea which circles had appeared where. I was fumbling around for an answer when I happened on Jenny's phone number. I'd had no intention of contacting her, but now it seemed imperative. I called the number and reached an irritable old woman who must have put the receiver down and gone about shouting for Jenny up and down the house. Finally Jenny's voice came on. "Yes?" she asked, as if surprised she should be receiving a call.

"Jenny, it's Father Wolfe, I met you on the train."

"The padre who almost missed his stop? What can I do for you?"

"I've become interested in your crop circles and I was wondering if you could show me one. Do you have a few hours available?"

"Hey, it's what I'm doing, I mean sure, is this afternoon cool?"

"Of course. I have a bicycle. I could meet you."

"I'm just down the lane. Number twenty-seven. Two o'clock?"

"Fine, fine. I'll be there."

After I hung up I was attacked by all sorts of anxieties. I told myself it was the only way of getting the necessary information, that Jenny could save me weeks of wandering about aimlessly. I silenced my anxieties as best I could and took off on the bicycle. She was waiting outside. She was wearing shorts and a Hawaiian shirt. I tried to look, well, priestly. She had a knapsack on her back and a map in her hand.

"Hi. We haven't much time today. Let's take a look at the closest. There's a new one, I hear, about fifteen minutes down this road. OK?" And she began to pedal up the road that ran past six or seven rows of houses and then into the countryside. Jenny set a very fast pace and I had to struggle to keep up. I pushed the old bike as fast as it would go, and I was relieved when she stopped and walked her bike the last hundred yards through a field to a stand of small trees.

"Let's leave the bikes here. We have to walk the rest of the way."

"Call me Gabriel."

"OK, Padre." She laughed. And took off into the field of rye. I followed, overwhelmed by the green beauty of the field that surrounded me. And the grass brushing against my thighs was an almost too pleasurable sensation. My shirt was soaked with sweat and I was breathing hard but not out of breath. Jenny stopped abruptly and I caught up with her. She was standing in a clearing, the diameter of which was at least thirty meters. She looked around for a moment and then paced off the diameter. I looked at the grass. It had been laid down in a clockwise pattern but without damaging the stalks. I looked closely at the perimeter, but the rye outside the circle seemed untouched. I stood very still but felt no peculiar sensations. I looked at Jenny across the circle. She had taken a camera out of her knapsack and was photographing, taking both close-ups and shots of the whole circle. She moved like a dancer, and the beauty of the afternoon and the odd stage on which we moved made it seem like ballet. I had to keep fighting a certain lightheadedness, yet everything was even more crystal clear than usual, defined in three dimensions. I was aware of my breath and that I was breathing rhythmically, and suddenly remembered being in Poncarelli's church and the curious hypnotic quality of the chanting. I sat down for a minute and Jenny came over with a flask. It was whiskey. I drank a few sips and handed it to her.

"I'm sorry," she said, "I should have warned you, but then very few folks fall under their spell." She gave me a strange look. There was almost shock, and a little wonder in it. The whiskey pulled me most of the way back to present time. I got up and looked at her for a moment. There was still that strange clarity of vision, the colors absolutely precise, as though my sense of sight had been cleansed. Jenny looked radiant, framed in the light, colors playing around her head. She gave me another drink from the flask and took one herself.

"Pull yourself together, you're starting to look happy." She laughed. "It's getting late and we've got a ride ahead of us. I'm not carrying you back to town."

When we reached the bicycles, Jenny hesitated a second. "You sure you're cool?"

I smiled. "I can ride, Jenny, I'm fine."

CHAPTER
ELEVEN

The whole episode had taken only about two hours, but time seemed to have been distorted along with my other senses. I was exhilarated and alarmed at the same time. I left Jenny at the lane leading to her pension with a promise to meet the next day. I was in a hurry to leave and she noticed it. I felt her stare after me as I bicycled home. I rushed into the rectory, checked the sauce I had left simmering, and then took a long, rather cold, shower. I felt strangely calm and relaxed. I found some paper and sat down and wrote a detailed description of everything that had taken place.

Father Dunstan arrived back about six. He burst into the house in what I was to learn was his customary fashion. "Smells Italian," he said, as he passed the kitchen. At half past seven we had a scotch and at eight we sat down to dinner. I served the pasta and a salad of dandelion greens I had found in the market. I had also found a bottle of inexpensive Chianti.

Dunstan ate in silence, then looked up to heaven. "Man does not live by curry alone. I see you found the town, Father. Did you discover any other local wonders while you were at it?"

"I went to see one of the crop circles that have been appearing in the neighborhood."

"Crop circles! What rot is this! Crop circles indeed." Dunstan attacked his pasta, head down, intent.

"It all seems pretty mysterious to me."

"Mystery is fine, if you admit it's a mystery and leave off, damn it. I can't go to town but some local stops me on the street and asks me what the Church thinks, or do I think they're caused by bloody wogs from space come to bugger our women. It's a pretty mystery I can tell you, but it doesn't seem to be a *Christian* mystery. And if they're spacemen, until they march up to the door and ask my opinion on the Virgin Birth or the mystery of transubstantiation, I'll have none of it. It's hard enough on the system to fail at melting the hard hearts of the English, let alone trying to convert some alien who's never even heard of Christ."

"Still, it would be interesting to find some explanation."

"If it would stop people from accosting me on the public street of the village, that would be fine. But when I'm finished understanding the Virgin Birth myself, I'll be ready to tackle other difficult-to-understand concepts." He took another enormous plate of pasta and refilled our glasses.

"But what do you think the Church's teaching should be on the matter?"

"Knowing Rome, they'll argue for years about how to baptize 'em, muck up their sex lives, tithe 'em, and make 'em feel guilty in the bargain."

I was enjoying this too much to let go of it. I wanted to bring Dunstan back to Rome with me and set him loose on the College of Cardinals. "Perhaps it's a hoax."

Dunstan paused, his fork halfway to his mouth. He spoke very seriously. "Father Wolfe," he said, "some are, surely. Couple of the boys hoisting their glasses at the pub decide to go trampling about in their neighbors' fields. But I've seen them, a few of them, and they're not manmade. Something very strange is happening and I don't think they're caused by pagan spacemen either. I don't bloody know, and you're getting to be like one of the old dowagers in the village, expecting me to know what nobody can know for sure." He got up and took our plates. "Good spaghetti, Gabriel."

I put all speculation to rest and went to bed. The gargoyles that appeared that night were sphinxlike with very prominent and beautiful breasts. I awoke the next morning with the sensation that I had been taken over a vast uncharted territory. For the first time since the dreams had begun, I could not remember the details of the journey, but was left with the unmistakable sexual feelings it engendered.

The sky was a uniform gray, timeless and static. My emotions were handfuls of mercury, at once poisonous and sensual, that shattered at the slightest touch. I walked the short distance to the church, unlocked it, and immediately was enveloped in the immense darkness. A few weak rays of light filtered down from the clerestory windows, which were fashioned out of a murky blue inferior stained glass. I tripped the master switch and was greeted by a few yellow shadows, nothing more. I retrieved the proper vestments and arranged them carefully on the green felt vesting table. I marked the correct passages in the enormous missal, opened the safe and found the box of hosts and the altar wine. Thank God, I thought, Dunstan had stopped using port. When everything was ready, I put the linen on, tied it with the cinch, kissed the stole, put it around my neck, and put on the ornate, heavy chasuble. I picked up the chalice and its coverings and went out to say Mass. I had always been able to concentrate during Mass, had found the ritual an immense source of comfort, a kind of cleansing. No matter what I felt, no matter what my mood or physical state, I was participating in an age-old rite of death, rebirth, and forgiveness. I could drop all my personae and simply be a priest performing the central mystery of my faith.

Memories of the day before came back, and I was aware of new meanings, new emphasis on certain phrases. *I will go unto the altar of God, to God who gives joy to my youth.* I could have spent days repeating those phrases, searching my life for the joy that always seemed to miss me. *This is my body. This is my blood, which has been shed for you.* I said the words of the transubstantiation slowly, and they made a physical sense to me for the first time. A sense not rooted in a theological reality, but in a reality of sinews, veins, organs, skin, gristle, bone, tissue.

No one noticed the care I took, the way I caressed each phrase. No one noticed that my voice almost broke a few times with emotion. No one noticed that my hands trembled slightly as I raised the host. *This is my body.* And since he was fully man, by the theologians' account, was he not preternaturally aware of his body, the exquisite intricacy of its movements, the pleasure of its presence, of all its functions? I had spent too much time meditating on the passions, the painful, unbearably cruel trial and death he had endured, and had never thought that he had for many years shared also the simple pleasures I never allowed myself to enjoy.

After Mass, I cleaned the sacristy, folded the vestments, and put them away. I took my time and savored each action, always conscious that it was still a part of the ritual, part of a precise and defined reality in which I was an integral part. I turned the lights off and locked up. Instead of going back to the rectory, I walked toward the center of the village, then turned to the right and walked for a long time up the road toward the fields. I walked rapidly and I was conscious not of my thoughts but just of my body, conscious of muscles stretching and contracting, of the cold held at bay by my exertions. And I noticed the patterns made by the branches of trees, noticed all the different shades of green. The visual world was new to me, a world that had never broken through the barrier of my thoughts.

CHAPTER TWELVE

After a hurried and solitary breakfast, I went back to my room and reread my notes, adding a few fresh thoughts. Then I bicycled to town to meet Jenny at a pub called the Ancient Oak. I sat down at a small table at the back of the dimly lit room with a pint of warm ale and waited. She arrived a few minutes later. I motioned to the barkeep and he brought another pint over to the table.

Jenny looked at me quizzically, and shook her head. "Padre, good to see you. I was wondering if you were just going to avoid me."

"Why would I do that?"

"Look, these crop circles are kind of *pagan*, you know what I mean? And I thought that might, like, mess you up a bit."

I smiled. "I admit it. They are troubling. I have no way—no context to begin to explain them."

"And there isn't much I can say that'll help. I'm an academic too, remember? And I don't understand either. But I don't worry about it. I'm gathering information about crop circles, and right now, if I don't understand, that's just fine. But you know, all the explanations are a little loony. UFOs, energy fields, you name it."

"Trying to find an explanation is like breathing to me. It's both instinctual and habitual. Habit reinforces instinct, or perhaps it's the other way around."

"But look," Jenny broke in, "you're a mystery man. Like what're you doing here, some high-power scholar at St. Jerold's, wandering in the fields? Something doesn't fit."

I felt the warmth of her concern, the physical warmth of it and I did not want to disappoint her. Her face had the clear untroubled look of one accustomed to her own truth, of one who is used to giving and receiving honestly. I could not shake the irony that both Jenny and Father Dunstan were responding with honesty and candor to a person who did not exist. I was even aware that I was beginning to allow feelings and experiences to happen to this fictional character. And if Father Wolfe began to live, what was to happen to Father D'Amato, the rising star of the Vatican, the Church's spy and henchman? What was to happen when this was over and I went back to solitude, when I went back to the arid corridors reeking of ambition, scandal, and gossip? I looked around and blinked, trying to take it in. I looked back at Jenny, her beautiful face with its deepening look of concern and even a hint of suspicion.

"I was sent here, it . . . is a kind of exile. I was teaching and preaching a set of principles and assumptions called . . . a philosophy that is currently out of favor with Rome. I am forbidden to preach or teach. St. Jerold's is certainly perfect in that regard."

Her face brightened. She whistled softly. "Jesus, Mary, and Joseph. You're practically an *outlaw*." She shook her head in disbelief. "If you're a renegade, how come you're so uptight? I thought you guys preach God is love and all that new-age stuff."

I laughed. "Not exactly. We are simply trying to give the Church a more realistic approach to political and social reality, not openly revolt against Church authority. I am still a Catholic theologian, an uptight Catholic theologian, if you will."

"I see. I'm beginning to see. But I gotta say, I'm no fan of the whole thing. I've been studying megalithic structures and pre-Christian history for years now. Chichén Itzá, Palenque, Machu Picchu. Stonehenge to

Egypt to Greece." Her expression became very serious again and she looked away to marshal her intellectual defenses. "Take the pre-Columbian civilizations. They were cooking along just fine for centuries. Their love of blood sacrifice is a little scary, but they had a going concern. Cortés shows up with a few padres in tow and in ten years most of the folks are dead and the rest are Catholic. A thousand years of art and religion gone forever to war, pestilence, and Catholicism. They try the same shit in Africa. Who were the savages, Padre?"

"I am not going to apologize for the excesses of Church history. That would take centuries. But there have also been heroic priests and nuns fighting for human rights and civil rights from Selma to South Africa."

"And they've had to fight their own authorities as well as the oppressors, right?"

"Well . . . yes."

"Why put up with it, Padre? Why take it? You're young and smart, uptight, sure, but that's not terminal. Why let 'em shut your mouth, when you know what they're always pulling?"

"Look, Jenny, there are other lessons of history, too. The Church has fought its way through schism and barely survived. It was madness. For a couple of centuries no one knew if their marriage was blessed by the right priest, if their children were really baptized. It was chaos. And today there are those who say the Church is too liberal and they are close to schism on the other side. We wish to influence Church policy from the inside, even if it takes time and there are a few casualties."

"You going to let yourself be a casualty?"

I smiled. "Ask Father Dunstan. At one time we would have faced torture and then been burned at the stake."

"I sure am *pleased* we are making progress."

"Progress of a kind. Progress is not a direct process. It dodges in and out of shadows. Circles around. Historians just try to straighten it into a line."

"You mean, maybe they'll burn you at the stake yet?" She laughed and tossed back the rest of her beer. "You're still a mystery, Padre, and a mystery you will remain. Maybe there is more here than you are saying, or maybe there is more here than you know." She got up and offered me her hand. "But I do enjoy talking to you. Most guys, well, you aren't most guys. In a coupla days I'm going to look at some more circles. Let me know if you can come along, OK?"

"I would like that."

"I'll fill the flask in case you get weird again."

I shook her hand and smiled. "Just give me a call."

I rode back to St. Jerold's quickly, my knuckles white on the handlebars, my jaw clamped shut. I put the bike away, unlocked the door to the church and went in. I didn't turn on any lights. Just sat in a back pew and looked blankly into the dreary shadows.

Inhibition is a life sentence, yet my adopted persona was allowing urges and impulses to surface. It was my first experience with the silvered reverse side of the mirror. I knew nothing of the self, knew nothing of psychology; it was not part of my training. If the wheel had not taken me in the direction it did, I would have avoided all knowledge of that mysterious *other*. In the mosaic of the wheel of fortune, the human figure hangs on to the wheel as it moves. And there is a frightening feeling of gravity, the feeling that an abyss yawns below him should he fall, an abyss from which there is no return. Sitting in the pew in the darkness of the centuries, I had the odd sensation of watching myself from an observer's position. As though it were happening in slow motion, I went over my conversations with Dunstan, went to see the crop circle with Jenny. I saw it all with a heightened sense of observation, because it was not as though these were my experiences. They were out of time. At any moment I might be called back to Rome, and Father Wolfe and his life would cease to exist. I could see no way in which these experiences would affect my ambitions, or break into my solitude.

I now know that was all illusory. The warmth and sympathy I elicited in my disguise were pleasurable experiences. But I thought these experiences were temporary, that the need for warmth and approval would disappear with the persona. When I became Father Wolfe, I took on his beliefs, his assumptions. But I did not see that the memories and emotions would be mine also.

A man is such a delicate mechanism. His manhood rests on such slender evidence. Unlike Dunstan, I had no faith to lose and therefore nothing to regain. The secret life of the intellect, the embodiment of the mark of solitude, the assertion of the rule of reason over the chaos of falsehood, the fastidious adherence to the details of a rigid behavioral code, the obeisance before a deity that rewarded goodness and punished evil were the pillars of my world. To admit doubt into this landscape was to court disaster. A man is defended by such meager armor, so thin it can be pierced by a look, a seemingly random series of events, by the implacable turning of the wheel. I think I began, alone in that dark church, to hate my defenses both for holding real experience away and for being so easily pierced by it.

CHAPTER THIRTEEN

That night as we were finishing Dunstan's disastrous attempt at English cooking, a meat pie and trifle for dessert, I asked again about his opinion on crop circles.

"Why are you so bloody interested?" he shot back.

"Because they seem to be genuinely interesting, and mysterious," I retorted. "You must have given them some thought, have spent a few moments in idle speculation."

"Idle speculation indeed. Are you up on your Druids, Gabriel? You know this whole area was very high on their list. Legend has it—mind, it's just legend—that St. Jerold's was built over a Druid shrine. Ritual sacrifice, strange initiation rites. All that pagan rot. But they did seem to have some real magic, and there is always something to their choice of places of power. Sometimes, walking out in the fields in the early morning after Mass, or just at sunset, I feel strange feelings and, now don't think I'm daft, I hear strange sounds. Never talked about it, never seemed unpleasant or threatening. Rather pleasurable actually. Makes a walk a bit more than exercise, less lonely.

"Maybe the old pagans had some strong magic that is still working. Or maybe they knew of some secret special properties of this area, strong magnetic forces. We moderns take the land, strip it, leave the hole and move someplace else with no bloody regard at all. All I know is the pagans worshiped here, and they worshiped the earth as a living being with magical properties that they desired to learn and manipulate. They were bloody-minded to be sure, but they were no fools."

"I admire your penchant for putting things in historical perspective, Brian."

"I am an old man, I have no other context to put things in. As some damn writer put it, all we really can say is that the incomprehensible is incomprehensible. Since the advent of the so-called scientific method, we have simply paved over the mysteries. So you are faced with a mystery here. Appreciate it, before you cut it to ribbons. It's not the only bit of magic in the world. And if it's sleight of hand, so much the better, we'll all have a good laugh and be done with it. Ah, but I see by the expression on your face that you consider it a personal affront, you're insulted if you can't find the answer." He threw his head back and laughed a laugh that turned slowly into a fit of coughing. Teary-eyed and red-faced he continued. "It's a joust, by God, your finely tuned overeducated intellect against the forces of nature or magic, or both. Lay on, I say, lay on."

His tone was so inclusive and jovial, I found it hard to take offense. Yet my situation made it difficult to laugh. "But you must see that as the story spreads, we will be called upon to present some explanation, if only to keep faith from being further eroded."

He began heavily, with a sigh from the depths, like a faint cry from the bottom of a mine shaft. "As I have said before, if the Church is interested in keeping faith from being eroded, they can surely start closer to home and with more important issues, eh, Gabriel?"

I wanted to shout that his nonexplanation might satisfy him, but my superiors would expect much more from me. I wanted to shout that I too had been touched by mysterious feelings. But all I said was, "Yes, of course, Brian, and it's not our problem one way or another."

The next days were a blur. I said Mass with the bitter taste of remorse in my mouth. I avoided contact, except the most formal and priestly. To the inhabitants of the village, I was as accepted as I would ever be. They considered me incapable of experience and I did nothing to prove them wrong. Soon I was myself again, and I felt free from troubling thoughts as though I had recovered from an illness that might have lingered had I not the strength of will to force it from my body.

Then Jenny called and invited me to look at another recent circle. I hesitated a moment, then accepted. I felt remote and confident, no longer vulnerable to the siren song of the Druids.

We met at noon and rode a few miles out of town, then turned off onto an unpaved service road. After riding a dusty mile or so, we stopped by an old oak. I was struck by the drama of its trunk and branches, its mass twisted and gnarled like an old man with a grisly secret.

We left the bicycles and trudged through the grass, which now reached almost to my waist. Jenny was wearing bluejeans and a gray sweatshirt. A leather bag with a long strap hung from her shoulder. The grass was very green and cool breezes swept over it. It was an ocean we waded through single file. We were at least a mile from a farmhouse that was little more than a stone square on a small rise above the wheat. The sky was windswept and clear although there were thunderheads poised on the horizon. I fought against the beauty of the day, the beauty of Jenny's form parting the way ahead of me. I believed if I fought against all impulses, all urges, I would be immune from the unexpected. Yet the wonder of the fields and the smells and the glory of a far-off hillside of wildflowers worked on me like a magician's spell.

Soon Jenny stopped, hesitated a moment, and then moved to her left about a hundred meters. When I caught up with her, she was on the edge of a circular track that was only a few meters wide. As in the other circle, the grain was not broken, but very carefully laid down. We crossed this track and made our way through twenty meters of grain to a huge circle at least two hundred meters in diameter.

Jenny whistled and said, "Jesus." She caught herself and looked at me. I looked around in disbelief at the great clockwise swirl of grain, at the shimmering sun-drenched patterns, at the breeze-inspired breathlike exhalations of the surrounding grain. "Jesus," I whispered.

I moved around the perimeter, focusing on the reality of it, focusing on the mathematics, on the physics, on whatever reasonable explanation might fit. I clung to the voice of science and reason even though I knew what I was witnessing was light-years away from a simple explanation. At some point I remember surrendering to another line of defense. I concentrated on the circle itself. I desired a logical explanation no less, but heeded Father Dunstan's advice. This is a mystery, I told myself, one of many in the universe. I am a simple human witness of the incomprehensible. The incomprehensible can be experienced without threatening the foundations of reason. This meditation made me feel better for at least a few minutes as I made my way around the circle. Jenny, moving the other way even more slowly, soon met me. She looked at me searchingly. Our eyes met in a gaze that lasted minutes.

It is a memory I relive often as I relive my history on the wheel. You must realize that a symptom of an inhibited self is the uneasiness with meeting anyone's gaze. I loved to stare, had a voyeuristic pleasure in it; yet it was painful when my gaze was met even for a moment. Inhibition cannot survive prolonged contact. The more rarefied the life, the less contact is necessary to turn the temple of inhibition into a crumbling ruin. I remember that look always. It has sustained me during times of universal censure and persecution.

I did not lose control, I did not reach out to embrace her, although when I replay the event in my mind, I do not think she would have turned away. Had I allowed it, that moment would have been sexual. It was not, at least not in a way that is usually described. It was the first time I felt anything spiritual, personally spiritual. I was transfixed by Jenny's radiance, by the way light seemed to gather around her, by her expression, which was serious but not without a hint of gentle mockery.

"Padre, I think this time I need the whiskey." Slowly, almost without taking her eyes away from mine, she turned and knelt and got the flask out of her bag. I knelt on one knee and took the flask when she offered it.

"You OK?" I asked.

"Fine, just fine." Her voice was small and sad. She took the flask back and took a long drink, shuddering slightly as she swallowed. We both sat down facing one another, the intimacy not awkward or embarrassing.

I looked down at the grain so neatly bent and laid flat. I looked up at the sky, watching the procession of clouds cast long shadows on the fields and the low hills beyond them. When I looked back at Jenny, she was crying, two tears making small tracks down her dark face. She caught one sob and let another out. I reached out and touched her hand.

"I'm all right," she managed and broke into sobs.

I turned to the side and she put her head against my shoulder and I put my arms around her shoulders and held her until her sobs subsided. She stayed there nestled against my shoulder. I remained very still and everything that was happening seemed right and for once I did not ask myself questions.

I do not know how long we sat there on the shimmering grasses of the mysterious, but then Jenny stood up, put both hands to her face, then let them fall to her side. I looked up at her but didn't move.

"You don't understand, don't *understand*."

"No."

"Run up here to bloody nowhere, to get away, get away from a very married professor, to get away from impossible men. Friends say, ain't nothing up there, no men, just nature. Just bloody boring nature. Run right up to something even more impossible. Sorry, Padre, I just got this weakness for uptight unavailable men. Not your fault. I mean you're cool, probably not uptight enough. Oh, I'm making a mess of this."

I handed her the flask. She sat down and drank.

I just looked at her. "Jenny, I . . ."

"You don't have to explain. Please don't explain. Pope told you not to preach, right? Let's just leave it part of the mystery. This happen to you often?"

"Never."

"Let's blame it on the circle, then."

"Dunstan says maybe they are leftover Druid magic."

"Dunstan is no fool."

"He says St. Jerold's is built on a Druid shrine, and this whole area had power for them."

"Then why is the Church gonna sell all this land to the Midlands Mining Company?"

"What are you talking about?"

"You mean you don't know?"

"Of course not."

"First time I saw you on the train, I thought you might be here to sell it for the Church."

"I had no idea. Dunstan has no idea either. How do you know?"

"Research is my job, remember? This leftover Druid land is going to get mined, stripped bare, and St. Jerold's with it. Some of us have been hoping the crop circle story would get out and stop the plans. But it's all moving too slow and the Church is moving too fast."

I was beginning to understand why I was sent. Assess the damage, gauge the situation, and develop scenarios. My superiors would think it a bonus if the crop circles disappeared. They never did want an explanation, only my report on how widespread was the belief in them. And they would expect me to have some idea of what to do about Dunstan.

"You OK, Padre? You look a little pale."

"I think we should probably be getting back."

"To reality?"

"I think we're there already."

CHAPTER
FOURTEEN

When I got back to St. Jerold's, I was exhausted and desired only a long bath and a scotch. I wished I believed in the power of prayer. I wished I believed in the wisdom of Rome. I wished I believed in the vow of celibacy. I wished I believed in liberation theology so I could be silent the rest of my life. I wished I believed that ambition was somehow worth the duplicity it required. Slipped under the door of my room was a telegram calling me to London to meet with Throckmorton and then back to Rome. Immediately.

I crumpled the telegram and threw it across the room. First things first, I reasoned. I headed back downstairs and poured myself a large scotch. Then I called the train station and made a reservation for the 10:12 to London the next day. I felt a wave of relief flow through me. I was afraid there might be a night train.

After a long bath and another drink, I was calm enough to think. To whom did I owe allegiance? To whom did I owe the truth, or even an explanation? How much power could I safely take and still keep control over the situation? Could I stop the sale of Church property and on what grounds? After considering these questions I settled for another drink. I looked fondly forward to the sin of drunkenness.

The evening was beginning to cast long shadows of the church spire over the rectory. I heard Dunstan come in and I could hear a general uproar in the kitchen. I sipped at the scotch and said good-bye to the landscape and began, reluctantly, to say good-bye to Father Wolfe.

I realized that neither the landscape nor Father Wolfe would exist much longer.

I called Jenny. "Jenny, it's Father Wolfe. I'm sorry but I'm afraid I've been called to Rome. I leave tomorrow. I didn't want you to think that this afternoon had anything to do with it."

"Padre, you're a real gentleman. It's going to be lonely here without you. Don't let them burn you at the stake, hear?"

"I promise. And I will see if I can do anything about the sale of the property. I've grown very fond of those fields. I've left my Rome address with Father Dunstan. Please write, and if there are any ruins in Rome that interest you, look me up."

"You've got a deal."

I finished the scotch and went down to help Dunstan with dinner. His idea of cooking was to bring everything to a good English boil and then add curry to it. If he destroyed the kitchen in the process so much the better.

"You receive the cable?" he asked.

"I've been called back to Rome immediately. I've no idea why."

"Perhaps they will lift their injunction."

"I doubt it. More likely they wish to send me somewhere even more remote."

"Impossible."

"I've heard talk in the village that this area is about to become less remote."

"You have, have you?"

"I understand that large parts of the county are about to be sold to the Midlands Mining Company."

"Dear God, where did you hear that?"

"I met a woman on the train, an anthropologist studying crop circles. I talked to her again a short time ago. She said she ran across the story doing research."

He was quiet for a long time. "I've feared this so long, it's a bit anticlimactic. I thought they would at least let me end my days here. It makes me wonder what the devil they'll do with me now. Maybe I'll just bloody hang on. Board myself up in the church, make them have at me with cranes and bulldozers."

It struck me that the thought had probably occurred to them also. "It's just a rumor. And even if it isn't, nothing will happen for a while. Sometimes obstacles appear. I'm stopping in London for a few days. I will try to investigate a little, try to see how serious they are."

"Oh, I'm sure they are serious. This church is a non-performing holding, better turned into ready cash. The few faithful won't cause much of a row, will they? Not against the million pounds this land will fetch. Create a few jobs hereabouts I dare say, even if the jobs are dangerous and bad for the health."

"What will you do?"

"Have a bit of family in Australia. They'll take me in, I think."

I see his face often as I struggle too with the results of fortune, as I struggle with the realization as he did at that moment that the wheel was finished with him, that no matter with what tenacity he clung to it, it would never begin another ascent. There was no bitterness in his face or manner, just the surrender of resignation. I could barely contain my revulsion. I looked around the room at the ancient flowered wallpaper blistered and cracked with age, at the threadbare carpet, at the frayed tablecloth, at the porcelain cups with their chips and hairline fractures.

I had come to admire Dunstan, but I refused to empathize with his position. It was too horrible. I felt trapped by the shabbiness of the situation and longed for the corridors of power and respect. It was the starch of newly laundered vestments I longed to touch, the perfect whiteness of altar cloth, the stiff bite of the Roman collar against my neck, the unyielding rigidity of the articles of faith that protected me against the mundane shabbiness of such a fate. I look back and see the heroic simplicity and human dignity in Dunstan's face and I weep for my inability to reach out to him. I felt that at any moment the floor would open in a wide yawn and I would be swallowed forever in the endless abyss of an unordered universe. I knew that it was my hand too that lit the pyre under Giordano Bruno, under Savonarola, and the myriad thousands broken on the rack and slaughtered so that I could worship the time-less order, the airless strictures of orthodoxy, the father-damaged and father-dominated law. It was I, too, who still ignored the truths of science and mathematics and clung to a world in which the heavens were hung on wires for the delight of man.

I wished to participate in the purity of that order and I understood the necessity of destroying any threat or compromise with that act of pure intelligence. I par-ticipated in it because, at every moment, I felt the pull of the vacuum. I feared the modern paradigm of the universe not because it posed another order, but be-cause at its heart it was so disorderly. It presumed a God of excess, a God more in love with chaos, a God asleep in the midst of a universe expanding out of control.

With panic I surveyed the room and closed my heart to Father Dunstan, because to allow the possibility of his fall from the wheel of fortune was to allow the pos-sibility of mine, was to allow that a fall from the wheel was a random act in a universe whose only principle was randomness, and that the pure intelligence that en-compassed the mind of God was in reality nothing more than dust dispersed through an abyss. I did not cling to the notion of an all-loving God, but rather to the idea of a God who had a plan, a special plan for my exis-tence, a plan that was not a cruel joke or an exercise in variables.

I realize now how right I was to fear that abyss. The vast uncharted reaches of chaos, worlds hurling them-selves toward annihilation, moonless vistas, seas of acid, methane sunsets, stars compressed to the size of a caper, stars that explode and vaporize whole solar systems, planets with no surface, planets of frozen gas, boundaries past which time and space cease to exist. The cold reality of the universe began to touch me that night. And I knew I was the lost brethren of the Inquisitors who tried to hold the world together against Copernicus, against Galileo, against Giordano Bruno. I was the brother of those who worshiped the perfect stasis, intricately embroidered chasubles which are the accumulated prayers of cloistered nuns, the Gothic vaults thrown as high as the dreams of the faithful of Chartres, the beaten gold of chalices, the impossibly ornate missals copied by the monkish masters of Cluny. I was the brother of those who saw the hand of the devil in the disorder of mysticism, of magic, of science. It was not faith that motivated them to torture and burn the unorthodox and the foreign. It was not the love of God that sent them over the globe clothing those who had no need of clothes, converting those who already believed in ancient and worthy gods. It was fear.

It was the fear that the earth might prove not to be the center and they might prove not to be the center of the world, the fear that all the prophecies might not point to them as the inheritors of power, the power to live in fear of the irrational, the mystical, the direct feminine link with the crucified body of Christ. "In the name of the Father" had always meant fear to me, the fear that could only be appeased with order, with acts done in the light.

This world is not the world of the male, it is the world delineated by the father. The male world is the world of youth and ascendancy, the world of the adventurer who ventures into the unknown, who competes for the female. The world of the father is the world that has already been conquered and must be held together with rigid, vengeful power lest it slip into the nether reaches of disorder. And out of my fear of disorder, I served the Church of the Father.

I don't remember much of what was said the rest of the evening. We talked of other matters. Or, I should say, Dunstan talked on and on about history. After we had cleaned up and had a final glass of sherry he presented me with a manuscript of his paper on Giordano Bruno.

"They couldn't silence Bruno, you know. His writings survive and his story. No one remembers his tormentors. No one remembers the name of the pope who burned him. But watch yourself, son. You know the final story of Bruno? There were a few choices they had, the bastards. They could have tortured him to death before they burned him. Apparently the executioner could be bribed to use dry wood instead of wet. Now dry wood flames up and robs the surrounding air of its oxygen and the poor bugger getting burned passes out before the flames get to him. Wet wood burns slowly and the victim stays alive while the flames scorch him. Our poor Bruno, of course, was burned alive with wet wood. So watch the bastards, Father Wolfe, and keep a bribe handy, you know what I mean?"

CHAPTER
FIFTEEN

The ride to London was obscured by depression. The sun was bright and the scenery bucolic but it was wasted on me. I longed for Rome and the comfort of intrigue. I arrived at Victoria Station in early afternoon. I treated myself to a cab and checked into the St. Regis Hotel, a few blocks from Trafalgar Square. I had a few hours to wait before my meeting with Throckmorton and I spent them wandering the streets. It was a wonderful walk: Hyde Park, Westminster, the Tower, but it was not Rome and I found my time spoiled by invidious comparisons. I found a pub and spent the last hour drinking warm beer and listening to what was supposed to be my first language. I understood very little of it.

I met Throckmorton at his club which was suitably old, suitably British, and stuffed with trophies which were now only echoes of empire. It seems they were able to cart away an enormous amount as they marched backward up the continents.

Throckmorton drew little from the promise of his name. He was tall and thin with a very thin and well-kept beard that had just begun to gray. He looked athletic in a sepulchral way, like a distance runner, and his eyes had that slightly dead and slightly deadly look that runners get.

"Father Wolfe, very pleased, very pleased." He didn't smile but winced in my direction. "Midlands Mining. I understand you've been in the neighborhood scouting about. I trust you found everything in order?"

"Not entirely."

He looked at me steadily, as though I were an opponent who had just pulled even with him. He led me into a small private study that looked as if Francis Bacon had just finished with it. Leather and rows of immense books. A table lit by a silver candelabrum that cast shadows over a late sixteenth-century globe and an astrolabe from about the same period. He drew me aside to a small table on which there was an ivory chessboard and pieces. We sat in eighteenth-century chairs that might have looked ostentatious in Versailles.

I recognized him as a kindred spirit and I despised him for it. He was clever and ruthless with a thick overlay of breeding to give him the illusion of gentility. He fingered the white queen in a proprietary manner and leveled his gaze at me. "Not entirely?"

"No. The fields you wish to develop employ local laborers and while a mining operation would employ more, although with modern techniques not many more, it would employ them in considerably more hazardous conditions. An existing church would be destroyed forever, something the combined forces of war, pestilence, and Protestant kings have been unable to do for ten centuries. Anyway, the publicity from environmentalists and crop circle investigators would create a major scandal. We cannot afford another major scandal."

While I was speaking, I watched the blood drain from his face as he registered my disdain and I watched it return in force as he reacted with anger. "Might I remind you, Father, the Church can afford a scandal, it is one of the few things it presently *can* afford. You must realize that the See has suffered of late, shall we say, some financial embarrassment, that the penchant of your fellow priests for buggering their parishioners is leaving a gaping hole in the books, that a few bank failures and Rome's reluctance to honor its letters of comfort have made it difficult to borrow. At great peril to my own position, I have negotiated the best possible deal for the See. We are prepared to pay more than the property is really worth, more than the Vatican might hope to gain from any other buyer. You were sent as an adviser, to help us gain information about the possible . . . public relations liabilities that might arise from these crop circles. You are speaking to me before you go back to Rome as a courtesy to *me*. If this deal goes awry, questions will be asked, questions for which I have no answers, or answers that will not stand careful scrutiny."

I replied with equal heat. "I was sent by Rome to investigate a phenomenon of interest to Rome. I was not given specific instructions. I found out about the sale quite by accident. If my superiors had other motives in their choice of assignments, they were not communicated to me. My report is to be given to my superiors and the decision of what to do with the information is theirs alone. I will not be intimidated or threatened. Good evening, Sir Henry." I stood to leave. He stood also, shaking with restrained fury.

"Father D'Amato, this is not what I was given to expect. I was told you were a realist. I have found your thinking exceedingly muddled and your position hopelessly naive. I hope the trip back to Rome will give you time enough to reconsider. I am sure you will learn that I am an excellent friend to my friends. Good-bye, Father."

As he walked me to the door I was struck by all the hides and pelts and mounted heads I passed. There were snow leopards, panthers, elephant-foot umbrella stands, polar bears, grizzly bears, antelope, and ibex with long black spiral horns. There were elaborate displays of exotic weapons, from Islamic daggers and medieval broadswords to crossbows and large-bore rifles. It made me realize that the club members had a highly developed sense of hunter and prey. Walking in silence down the halls on Persian runners, walls lined with trophies of every sort, I had the feeling I might suddenly cross the line between guest and hunted. Throckmorton stalked down the aisle at my side, looking neither right nor left. He opened the door and I went out into the chill London night.

I walked around for a while, trying to clear my head. I was not angry, and at that point I did not feel threatened, at least not by Throckmorton. I was troubled and worried at having been used as a pawn in what was increasingly a dangerous game. There were numerous shadowy lay organizations that worked to advance Church programs, and while they might strut around making themselves seem powerful, the hierarchy treated them as blunt instruments. I tried to think clearly, to assess my position. I was sent to investigate and to deliver a report. That was what I would do. All I could do.

My thoughts moved on to Giordano Bruno. He, after all, had become prey at some point, lured back to Italy, back to Venice and then delivered into the hands of the Inquisition. In Dunstan's account it was really pride that lured him back, pride and political revolution. Apparently he acted on the advice of astrological charts that foretold great changes at the turn of the century. Of course he was burned in 1600, burned by a hierarchy who had perhaps been reading the same charts and who were willing to spare no expense to see that the old order remained. The old order which always seems to remain. I, and those like me, make sure of that.

CHAPTER SIXTEEN

I stayed in my room most of the next day and drank tea while I prepared my report. I used every trick of rhetoric and sophistry I knew. I embellished like a craftsman who brings up just the right luster to obscure his forgery, neither making it so bright it calls attention to its brightness, nor so dim that it hides its brilliance. The report was crafted so that all the conclusions became obvious but would appear to be arrived at by the reader and not the author. I had never loved the gift of scholarship so well. I was so taken with my arguments I began to believe them myself.

I flew into Da Vinci the next afternoon. It was raining and the streets of Rome were swept with water. The train left me at the Trastevere station and I took a cab to the front of Santa Maria del Valle. I tipped the driver enough to ensure he wouldn't drive off and walked the short distance to the Campo dei Fiori. It was empty in the rain, the flower sellers and vegetable farmers who make their living in the shadow of Giordano Bruno's statue having long since taken refuge in the small bars that line the ancient piazza. His cowled form towered above me.

I returned to the cab which took me up the Corso, across the Tiber, and around St. Peter's to the entrance of its offices and the inner reaches of its power. I entered, examining my conscience as though I were guilty of some great transgression. I walked quickly over the marble, my steps punctuated by the swish of my cassock.

Monsignor Signorelli was waiting for me exactly where I had left him. He barely glanced up from the dossier he was reading. I handed him my report and I was relieved that I no longer had an option. He did not look up, but kept reading. I stood there at a kind of priestly attention until he motioned for me to go.

I walked back to my apartment near the Gianicolo, watered the few plants that remained alive, and looked briefly at a prodigious stack of mail. But there were no interesting postmarks and I read through it aware that the solitude I once savored tasted of the stagnant air of loneliness.

For a few days I busied myself with cleaning up the accumulated stacks of interstaff memos and reports. Normally it would have only taken forty-five minutes, but an absence of a few weeks made even a cursory perusal take considerably longer. It seemed as though I had been away an eternity. The mountain of paperwork did nothing to improve my disposition.

The reports ranged from the bizarre to the fantastic. My colleagues were thorough and internationalist. From Brazil came a report of a quasi-Catholic cult of healers claiming to cure everything from cancer to AIDS with a combination of prayer rituals, macumba, and psychosurgery imported from the Philippines. From Central America, a chilling study about how fundamentalists were making huge inroads on traditionally Catholic cultures with grass-roots organizing among peasants, for generations ignored by the Church hierarchy. From Africa, results of surveillance on a truly saintly healer, a bishop who had inspired distrust with his gentle, loving manner and his habit of healing everyone who came to him free of charge. From Texas, the story of rosaries turning to gold, of a mass hallucination where the sun seemed to spin perilously close to the earth, straining credulity as well as four centuries of physics. Strange how old ideas die. From Yugoslavia, the sad end to a ten-year visitation story as the whole region convulsed in civil war.

It interested me that the Virgin had been warning Yugoslavs for years against impending disaster should they not forsake their private hatreds. She had chosen the young children of Madjugorie, as she had chosen the children of Fatima before World War I. The children had listened and learned and pilgrims gathered and watched when they should have listened and learned. The pilgrims went back to conventional lives, their spirits momentarily lifted, their prim orthodoxies confirmed, when in reality the Virgin had been warning them not of personal damnation but of the very real political danger should they not turn back from nationalist and tribalist horror. The Yugoslavs, like other Europeans before them, if they heard at all, heard only of their private sins, their paltry and meaningless sensual writhings, their uncontrolled desire for another glass of wine, or for their neighbor's wife or his money, not thinking of the huge map of carnage that awaited them collectively. And the Church buried its warnings in the sickeningly repressive rhetoric with which it tried to stage-manage the tensions for its own provincial gain. All over the world with increasing fervor the omens were appearing and receiving brief and sensationalist attention, followed by complete misunderstanding and then amnesia.

Had I not been ambitious, with the instinct of an animal searching for higher ground before a flood, I would have desired nothing more than the monastery where perfect order could be had at the cost of the more worldly values I was addicted to no less than the drunkard his bottle. The drunk or drug addict runs the risk of destroying his body, his mind, and his spirit. He participates in the corruption that surrounds their supply and distribution. But addiction to power, to greed, to acquisition, to the violence and destruction of war—these threaten the life of the planet and are rewarded at every turn.

Out of the depths, warnings surfaced. I too ignored them, mistaking them as threats to my comfortable existence, as threats to the stern Father with whom I aligned myself. I did not run to the monastery and end my days and this story in prayer and contemplation. I cleared my desk and dutifully awaited the disposition of my report and the personal reward or punishment it might garner. I became fastidious, taking long showers and changing my cassock two or three times a day. I cleaned and cleaned my apartment. I was distraught until my desk was empty and all my papers filed.

I took the same walk every day at exactly the same time. Invariably I made my way down the hill into Trastevere, skirting the plaintive shouts of the inmates of the Maria Coeli prison, skirting the bucolic splendor of the botanical gardens, skirting the beautiful Renaissance villas built on grounds that ages before had belonged to Julius Caesar and bequeathed by him to the people of Rome. I walked across the Ponte Sisto and up the warren of narrow ancient streets to the Campo where I inevitably stood at the feet of Giordano Bruno, my opposite, my brother.

My dreams dragged me over the streets torn apart by civil war, the streets of Beirut, of Dubrovnik, of San Salvador. Through deserted streets strewn with rubble, through Tiananmen Square after the tanks had churned the pavement with their treads, through Rangoon after the demonstrations, through Basra, through Baghdad, its streets loud with the cries of starving children. The more I tried in my everyday life to control, to ritualize, to codify my behavior as a charm against anxiety, the more detailed and explicit became my dreams.

As I stood under the statue of Bruno I stretched myself to understand him, to understand how he came to the conclusion in the 1580s and '90s that there were innumerable worlds, how he sought to expand God to hold real immensity rather than manage him in service of the finite. I longed to dive into his mind, into a magical sense of a Christian universe without boundary. I wanted to understand his desire for subversion, the belief that he could help to usher in an age of reform and spiritual awakening. I fell so short, and it humbled me.

Finally I was called to Monsignor Signorelli's office. After being kept waiting the ritual half-hour I was ushered into his office by his ancient secretary, who, like Signorelli, had always been there, and looked as though he were past his prime when Leo X ruled. Signorelli gestured me to be seated and I obeyed. He took a few long minutes to finish reading a letter and another few to put it away, and another few minutes to fold his hands on his desk.

"So, Father D'Amato, what is this business with crop circles and what is this business with Signor Throckmorton?" He looked at me as if from a great height, as if he could barely see me, as if I had that little right to exist at all, to ruffle the surface of his reality.

"The circles, Monsignor," I began, "have little to do with us if we are careful. They appear and, as phenomena, they call attention to themselves. The groundswell of interest is growing. If we call attention to them ourselves by selling the fields, the possibility of long-range damage to our interests is great indeed. Let me add that I found out about the proposed sale in the course of my investigation. The Holy See did not see fit to inform me of the real purpose of my mission and put me in a situation that might have proved embarrassing for everyone. Lord Throckmorton demanded my cooperation, and beneath that demand I sensed his unease about any investigation into the 'extravagant' price he negotiated for us."

Signorelli looked at me for a long time. His gaze came closer and more threatening. Finally he grunted and said, "What about Dunstan?"

"Father Dunstan is an old man. He busies himself with harmless scholarship and the management of a small parish. He is better left alone. It is all better left alone."

Another long pause.

When Signorelli finally spoke, there was a hint of amusement and sarcasm in his voice. What might have been the beginnings of a smile played on his lips. "Father D'Amato. There was reason for our actions. Up until now our information has been controlled by people close to Throckmorton. He has great influence. Although he commands more fear than respect, the result is the same. Those close to him tend to act in accordance with his stated or unstated wishes. We needed an outside opinion. Had we openly sent an appraisal team, we risked his attempting to suborn or discredit its results. Our office provided the necessary cover. One man who could keep his eyes open and his wits about him. Of course, we knew Throckmorton would be informed and therefore it was necessary to have you meet and speak with him. Had you been briefed, he might have sensed it and been alarmed rather than just angry. He is not a pleasant man when alarmed.

"Your assessment was, however, accurate. We have spent the days since your return investigating. A very careful but plodding process. Sir Henry Throckmorton, it seems, is playing a very complicated game. He made us think he had arranged a price favorable to the Holy See. In reality, he planned to enrich himself at our expense. Through his contacts at Whitehall, he had learned that the British government has a long-range plan to develop that region. All he had to do was wait and when the plan was announced next year, after a sufficient time for our memories to be dulled by other matters, the value of the land would triple and Throckmorton, who, through his financial sleight of hand now owns controlling interest in Midlands Mining, would be a very rich man. If I might say so, it was a brilliant ploy.

"Our plan now is to back out of the deal on some pretext and to await quietly the Crown's prospectus, which will not even reach the preliminary stages for a few years. Perhaps St. Jerold's will once more become an asset, yes?

"Now it seems your specific talents are needed elsewhere. Your efforts in this matter will not go unnoticed.

Come and see me at eleven tomorrow and be prepared for another small trip. *Buon giorno*, Father."

I made a perfunctory but respectful bow and left.

I walked the corridors of the Vatican aimlessly, passing from one frescoed gallery to another, finding myself finally and inexplicably in the Corridor of Maps. There was a crush of tourists on their way to view the restored Sistine Chapel. I could barely move or breathe as I was borne along on a human tide that crested when it reached the chapel. The chapel itself was awash with people standing silently with their heads craning upward to look at the ceiling, restored now to the brilliance it had the day Michelangelo finished it. Even though they were silent, there was a constant background of murmuring sound, the sounds pebbles might make when they are dragged back into the ocean by a strong undercurrent. Almost against my will I looked up with them.

I was taught to be in such awe of the technical undertaking, of the artistic daring, that like most I had never really looked at the content of the composition. What I saw brought back echoes of Dunstan's paper on Giordano Bruno.

Bruno had been a Renaissance Magus, interested in Christianity as a continuous thread of revelation that reached all the way to ancient Egypt. And here it was again in the Sistine Chapel. I was riveted by the massive frescoes of the sibyls, each receiving and writing a prediction that foretold the Christian era. These were not merely references to Old Testament prophecy but to the connections that Christianity had to classical pagan prophets. Bruno was more interested in the thread of mystical and magical religion than in Catholic orthodoxy. And so it seemed was Michelangelo.

I had realized long before that the Sistine Chapel was not a holy place, that in fact it had been painted for a pope who was a libertine, a brilliant general, and perhaps barely Christian at all. But Julius was learned and perhaps also interested in paganizing Catholicism rather than converting the heathens. In the graceful folds of the sibyls' tunics, the master painter had encoded a puzzle, the solution of which has eluded us. Classical antiquity had reemerged in the Renaissance, and it was necessary to create a mystical lineage outside the Old Testament predictions. It was necessary to prove that the Greeks and the Persians and the Egyptians had a history that foretold the Christian era and thereby liberate art and culture from the confines of scripture. The sibyls were proof that an extra-biblical tradition existed and argued for a mysticism that flourished outside the Judeo-Christian world. Like Bruno, Michelangelo was depicting a universal mystical process that included the sibyls, as Bruno had included the Egyptians.

I was a man without convictions, philosophy, or scruples. I was a man being dragged against his will into the acknowledgment of mystical forces outside the Church or any church. I knew nothing of these forces except that they were destroying the underpinnings of my narrow world. What was my place, my position, but to enforce the rule of reason and authority in a world haplessly adrift without them? And while I had been successful in protecting the interests of the Church, I had been less successful in shielding my own. I was alone in a hostile world sworn to protect the interests of an institution which could no longer protect me from myself. I wondered what it was to be a man, a man apart from the role I had adopted with such vehemence and self-protective zeal. And with the beautiful face of the Thracian sibyl before me I vowed to investigate the mystical thread that was so secretly woven through the centuries.

CHAPTER
SEVENTEEN

Everything was on fire. The tapestries, the tables of in-
laid wood, the cabinets that housed jewel-encrusted
chalices, the ancient vestments woven with gold thread
from stolen Inca treasures—everything was on fire. The
maps of the world, illuminated manuscripts, all the
paintings of the Annunciation were burning, and a grin-
ning beast carried me through flames that threatened
to incinerate time itself. I awoke in the first glow of
morning. I dressed hurriedly, but not in clerical robes.

My superiors misjudged me as badly as I misjudged
myself. They thought there were no questions that
might tempt me, that my heartbeat was only a way of
counting time, and time was only a canvas upon which
my destiny would be revealed. I did not even have to
barter my soul in the service of my ambition, I only had
to refuse to use it, to stifle its urges, to inhibit its demands upon my desires.

They thought I could touch a mystical world in their
service and not come away changed. But what of the
few that touched me either with the sincerity of their
quests or the authenticity of their experiences? What
of them? I was supposed to be immune from the touch
of mystery, I was supposed to protect the orderly practices of an institution from the process that created it.

As I wandered, I noticed that I no longer inspired
instant respect and acceptance. Dressed as a priest,
the world came to me. I could receive it, could control
its demands and judge its shortcomings. To learn to
be a man it would be necessary to touch sorrow and

pleasure, not wait for a priest's portion to be delivered to me.

I went to the Vatican the next day to see Monsignor Signorelli but he was not in his office, an occurrence so unusual as to be unbelievable. His secretary murmured something about an emergency meeting and suggested I return the next day. I wandered about Vatican City fighting off a strange foreboding. Cold had swept down from the north and invaded my bones. I walked over the bridge toward the tomb of Augustus. A sky of slag, of smothering damp grayness, oppressed me. I walked faster but with no direction. Down the Spanish Steps, the Via Condotti, past all the gleaming shops, past the Colonna with its relief depicting past and forgotten glory, to the Piazza Navona where the caricaturists and watercolorists and prostitutes and pickpockets were all gathering their props and scurrying away as the rain slanted toward them, and into the Bar della Pace where I drank a lonely brandy in no one's honor and then finally ducked into the small Santa Maria della Pace at the end of the street. I felt like an outsider, a confused and anxious man in a space of harmony and peace. I looked up to find the sibyls again, this time Raphael's. The Renaissance masters had used the image of the sibyls not only to link Christianity to a magical past but to point the way to the future. And I wondered as I stared at the beauty and peacefulness of the della Pace sibyls if there was not in their faces a warning.

CHAPTER EIGHTEEN

"Sit down, Father Gabriel, sit down." Monsignor Signorelli was uncommonly jovial and this added to my uneasiness.

"Much is happening, too much. As you know, the last ten years have seen an increase in the number of apparitions of the Virgin Mary. Although there has been relative calm since you have been with us, the Virgin has been showing up in many of the troubled places in the world, places where we have enough trouble already. Protestant fundamentalists on one side and liberationists on the other. And the Virgin appears where and when she wills. She never has had a firm grasp on cold war politics, has she? Now with the cold war over and regional conflicts on the rise, she makes even more unscheduled and disturbing visits. I must tell you the situation is very serious. Even when she appears in isolated places, even when we are there with our investigators, with our rational explanations, interest grows as word gets around on the blasted CNN. As you know, even in the relative obscurity of Fatima, within weeks, tens of thousands followed the children to their apparitions. Also as you know, ten million have made their way to Madjugorie. With the millennium approaching, it seems everyone is looking for a sign, a signal, a miracle.

"I could not see you yesterday because I was in meetings all day with a curial committee. It seems that Mary has been very busy lately. And in your native country.

"With great care and diplomacy, we have kept the

American Church under control. They seem to have as much passion for individualism and democracy as they do for materialism and capitalism. Also, their penchant for championing racial equality and human rights in every country but their own and their growing acceptance of the complete equality of women disturb us. The way they defy Rome on the issues of birth control and social activism threatens the very foundations of our authority. So far we have contained these threats. But if a cult of Mary springs up and draws all the disparate elements together, no amount of inquisitorial zeal will staunch the wound it will create.

"Your next assignment takes you to your home country, to a place in California I have never heard of, Point Reyes Station. It is too small to appear on any of our maps. Which would make it seem that it is too small to do us any harm. But you will be arriving, probably with the first reporters and film crews. It is a rapidly developing apparition episode, with potentially the same impact as a Fatima or Lourdes. Your assignment is to control its impact. You must use our influence to deflect media attention before it becomes an international incident. Do I make myself clear?"

"Monsignor," I almost shouted, "what you ask is impossible for a priest. The American press has rarely had its arm twisted except by Spellman, Cody, or O'Connor. A mere priest will not last until noon. It will take authority, which means money and the raw intelligence to back it up. It means applying pressure from the top down. How many divisions did you say we had?"

"We are not fools, Father D'Amato. You will, of course, have both the means and the intelligence to do what is necessary. And you will be traveling in disguise, but"—and here a rictus of pain moved over his face like a small electrocution—"not like the last time. This trip you will be given . . . the robes of a bishop, a bishop attached to the office of the Nuncio. You will see Father Anastasius, he has the proper attire ready.

"Let me caution you. You will dress and comport

yourself as a bishop of the Roman Church. You will keep us informed of your progress, and the means to accomplish your ends will be made available to you. But you have not been consecrated a bishop, you will not abuse your temporary status, and you will take great care that you do not inspire anyone to check deeply into your background. Is that understood?"

"It is understood. God help me if I fail."

"Father D'Amato, not even God will help you if you fail."

CHAPTER
NINETEEN

I arrived in San Francisco on a day obscured by smoke. It was late spring of an indeterminate season during an interminable drought. I was met at the airport by Emilio, a young Hispanic who had been assigned to be my driver. The first time he called me "excellency" I almost looked around to see whom he was addressing. He ushered me through the airport and into the backseat of the longest and most ostentatious automobile I had ever seen. If this is the custom of Vatican diplomats, I thought, it was no wonder the Church was going broke. But I sank back into the leather cushions for the drive into the city.

I was astounded. After exiting a freeway choked with oversize automobiles, we glided up Seventh Street toward Market in the silent white behemoth with tinted windows. I saw hundreds of men and women, women with children, all of them in rags, pushing shopping carts slowly up and down the sidewalks that were now their homes. Groups of men stood at the corners with a look of despair branded into their weather-beaten faces. Everything seemed to move in slow motion. No one moved with a sense of purpose or destination. I was not prepared for such human misery and degradation.

In Italy, in Rome, the government is riddled with corruption, nepotism, and labyrinthine bureaucratic machinations. Yet in Rome at its worst, at its most inept, a scene like this was impossible to imagine. Nor was the irony of my position lost on me. The wheel of fortune had placed me in a position of power which in-sulated me from poverty and anarchy. I was just pass-ing through, silently peering out through tinted lenses at the colossal failure of a civilization. The part of me that had begun to feel the faint stirrings of spirituality wanted to stop the car, get out and walk among these souls as Francis would have. The part of me that was trapped, imprisoned in purple, yoked by the stiff white collar, shrouded in expensively tailored robes, felt noth-ing but relief and the furthest feeling from compassion.

I had a role to play and a secret mission to carry out. I was to do the bidding of the Father, to ensure that order and reason were not compromised. One thing was apparent, however. I saw no other priest walking among these people ministering to their needs. I saw no Fran-ciscan, inspired by his founder, feeding and clothing his flock, offering them shelter and sanctuary in his cav-ernous and empty church.

I remembered Poncarelli and my heart ached for the part I had played in his exile. And I shook with dread at the part I was to play now. Does every heart beat with such divisive systole and diastole? Does every heart reach out and pull back almost at the same time?

This moral crisis was mercifully brief. Soon we en-tered the shadow of a modern hotel with a giant glass scallop shell. From there we entered a forest of towers, like the towers erected by the just of San Gimignano simply to prove their wealth and moral superiority. Here the streets were filled with Medici, lending and buying, their gaits infused with purpose, confidence, and utter ruthlessness. I relaxed. I was among my own. Emilio guided his monstrosity into the cool depths below the cathedral, which rose in one sweeping mass to dominate its portion of skyline.

"This way, excellency." Emilio carried my suitcases and I followed. The cathedral rectory was resplendent in an understated way. It reeked of privilege and celi-bate comfort. It was a fortress blocking out the wails of the people, the grace and warmth of the feminine, and the muscular posturing of the male. It smelled of the precise and empty lair of the Father.

"This way, excellency." Emilio led me to a room that was more like a suite in an expensive hotel. Heavy beige drapes opened slightly to reveal a stunning view of the bay. Sailboats with billowing spinnakers crossed each others' wakes in abstract and leisurely patterns.

There was a leather sofa with matching chairs and an immense desk. Emilio set my suitcases down and stood silently for a moment awaiting further orders. He was slender, of medium height, with dark Indian features and a permanently wary look.

"Where will you be, if I need to go out?"

"Excellency, just dial six on your telephone."

I went to the window and looked out over the city. I could see Coit Tower, the Pyramid, Alcatraz, the Golden Gate. The postcard city, the city you pay to see from the hilltops. Just enough breeze had blown up to keep the haze from obscuring the view. I went over to the desk but its size and emptiness blocked my thoughts so I sank into a leather chair and began to read about the Virgin of Point Reyes Station.

A young Mexican girl, as irony would have it named Guadalupe, started seeing apparitions of the Virgin on a cliff overlooking the immense stretch of deserted beach that is the Point Reyes National Seashore. She went up there with her brothers who fed horses and tended cattle for a local rancher, a Pietro Giaquinto. She made a small shrine there and put fresh flowers on it every few days. About a month later the Virgin appeared to her, calling her name.

She talked of her apparition to her mother, who told the parish priest. The priest talked to the girl, who readily told him the story. The Virgin was beautiful and spoke her name in Spanish. Guadalupe didn't see anything unusual about being visited by the Virgin.

But then one Friday, Guadalupe was out on the cliff tending her shrine when three Anglo women happened by. Guadalupe was a little frightened but went about her business of putting fresh roses before the statue. The Virgin appeared to her and she went into a trance-like state, her neck craning up at an odd angle. The women noticed her. They claimed afterward that they saw a strange light suffuse the girl and that she was able to maintain her body in this ecstatic position for many minutes.

After the Virgin disappeared, Guadalupe fainted, and the women took care of her until she regained con-sciousness. Then they drove her back to town and told the priest what they had seen. The next day there was a small group of women. The next, a small crowd.

The shrine at the ranch was now tended as a beau-tiful garden. Wildflowers bloom on the slope behind it. Someone built a small wooden structure over the statue. The weekly visits now included about eighty women. A small article appeared in the *Point Reyes Light* and was seen by a tourist whose cousin was a member of the Fatima Society, which attempts to monitor apparitions worldwide. It was a short leap of faxes before the news and ramifications reached my superiors.

CHAPTER
TWENTY

The next morning Emilio and I drove out to Point Reyes. The ride through the hills of Marin County was beautiful. There had been just enough rain to turn the hills emerald green, although the streams were already dry. Point Reyes Station consisted of a bakery, a hardware store, a cowboy bar, and a few restaurants. As a community it was sleepy and, except for weekends, when tourists rolled through on their way to the ocean or to one of the many expensive inns, tranquil.

The fog had just cleared as we arrived and a cool breeze blew down the main street, which was deserted except for a small clot of people clustered around the bakery sipping coffee. A small jolt of apprehension went through me. A bishop was as out of place here as a crow in a formation of geese. I said a small prayer of thanks that I had been able to jettison the limousine before I left San Francisco.

St. Anne's was a mile outside Point Reyes, a small church built just after the time churches, filling stations, and banks began to share the same utilitarian architecture. The whole church would have been dwarfed by the smallest side altar of St. Peter's. The rectory was a simple two-story house next door. Because it was overcrowded to begin with, I would be staying in a small inn on the other side of town.

Emilio and I walked up the stairs to the rectory and were greeted immediately by Father Thomas O'Meara, a tall, gaunt man with thinning hair and a bony, fleshless face that just missed being sinister. A faint smile crossed his face. "Your excellency, come in, come in."

He led us into a small living room where Fathers Richard Helm and Garcia Riccardo were seated on an old couch. The room had that spartan clutter that all places acquire when lonely men pass through them. Father Helm couldn't have been much over thirty. He was short and fat and carried his weight with embarrassment. Father Riccardo was small and slender. His hair had begun to gray but his face still looked youthful. He seemed frightened and ill at ease. They all seemed frightened and ill at ease. A representative of the Vatican elicited a universal response.

I asked them to explain, but all they could manage was an hour's worth of self-justification. I learned very little except that they had been deluged with questions for which they had no answers, and that so far the media had stayed away.

When I left them they were sullen and angry and I was tired and thirsty. Emilio drove me to the Estero, an elegant inn with a spectacular view of Tomales Bay. I had made arrangements to use one of the cars that belonged to the rectory and dismissed Emilio back to the city.

My suite at the Estero was actually a small detached house with a bedroom, bath, and kitchen. The refrigerator was stocked with a few necessities and I had a bottle of scotch in my suitcase.

I fixed myself a drink and walked out into the cool evening air. As I looked out over the incomparable beauty, I felt a sudden chill. There were no words attached to the feeling, it was just a moment, a wave that washed over me leaving me utterly alone on a desolate ecclesiastic beach. Somewhere out in the mists a young girl struggled with a visitation that had shattered her youth into pieces. What else would break apart before it all receded into the past?

What of the miraculous? Gabriel the Apostate, of course, had trouble believing in the miraculous. He was a modern man, even if he clung to, gave lip service to, ideas that were prescientific. But what of that? Did not everyone still refer to sunrise and sunset, even though the ashes of Bruno were still smoldering when we all agreed finally that the earth revolved around the sun? Do not millions still subscribe to astrology, even though the ancient symbols comprise stars which are billions of light-years from one another? So what if poor Gabriel, the *counterfeit* bishop, the false shepherd who sets out to scatter the sheep in all directions—so what if he is able to explain in the finest rhetoric the concept of the Trinity, reconcile Genesis with Darwin, Joshua with Galileo, Augustine with Freud? So what if he knew all the while that, taken together, the concepts of Catholicism were preposterous, beginning with original sin and ending with the resurrection of the body?

There has always been a difference between believing in the Virgin Birth, the Resurrection, the Immaculate Conception, the Ascension, the Assumption, and other feats that suspend the laws of physics and actually witnessing the manifestations themselves. Before me in space and time lay the unknown. Gabriel the Apostate drank another scotch and then another, hoping the whiskey might return him to his arrogant belief in the power of his office and in the organization which depended on him and on others like him for its smooth operation.

I slept late the next morning and awoke to knocking at my door. I dressed hurriedly and greeted the owner of the Estero, a small, slight woman in her late forties, dressed in a rose-colored silk shirt and wool slacks. One pair of eyeglasses perched precariously on her head and another, on a silver chain, rested on her chest. She squinted at me and pursed her lips.

"Excuse me, excuse, me," she intoned like a curial prelate beginning a long sermon. "But someone dropped off a car for you this morning and it's blocking the drive. Could you move it? I mean I don't want to disturb you but I have a lot to do. I'm not well, haven't been for years, and I have a massage at ten and a chiropractor at eleven. The town's going crazy, let me tell you. Hardly a room left. A friend who does tarot just called me and said a bunch of women are out at the shrine. Everyone feels the vibes, you know. Anyway, I've got to go. My allergies are kicking up, a bad season for me." She squinted at me again, pursed her lips even tighter, turned abruptly, and disappeared through a small gate that was almost hidden in a hedge.

I dressed in a bishop's black suit with the magisterial touches of purple, and grabbed a cup of coffee at the bakery. My head hurt and the coffee was too weak. I felt off balance and irritable. I stopped at a gas station and got directions, then headed for Kehoe Beach. The small parking area was choked with cars and I had to park about a half mile down the road. The hills were covered with wildflowers. I joined a line of women following a narrow trail toward Mary's shrine. I looked around as I walked. Below me was a marsh where tall reeds waved in the breeze. Beyond was a large dune and I could hear waves crashing on the shore. There must have been a hundred women crowded around the shrine. Everyone eyed me suspiciously. I moved slowly toward the circle and stood next to two young women who were deep in conversation. They were huddled together and spoke in whispers that barely carried over the sound of the surf.

"Where's Guadalupe? Nobody's seen her for days. They say she never comes here anymore. Someone told me Father O'Meara told her to stop talking nonsense and to stay away from the shrine."

"Sandy told me that Guadalupe's scared, scared of the attention she's getting, scared her brothers will lose their jobs with Giaquinto, scared of the Anglo priests."

"Well, if I were her, I'd be scared too. She's just a girl and Suzanne says she's bright, but has always been extremely withdrawn. Now she hardly says a word."

I moved off and stood alone for a few minutes. On a small hill that overlooked the shrine were two large stakebed trucks with GIAQUINTO DAIRY stenciled on the doors. Three men stood talking to one another. A few yards off an older man stood and stared at the shrine and the ever-growing circle around it.

I walked back down the hill. It was about eleven and my head throbbed. The sun broke through the fog then and bathed the scene in brilliant sunlight. The sound of the rosary said in unison mixed with the sound of the surf as I walked the narrow path that led to the beach.

It took about half an hour to get to the ocean along a muddy path that ended in a sand dune. I clambered up the dune and scrambled down the other side. Waves crashed against miles of deserted beach. The violence and desolation were like a tonic and soon my head cleared. I found a piece of driftwood for a walking stick and walked peacefully up the beach. I stopped after about a mile to admire what appeared to be a pictograph-like figure which had been carved by wind and ocean on the face of the sandstone cliff.

At the base of the cliff were small dunes covered with reeds that stood four or five feet tall, and behind the reeds a small row of shallow caves. I was intrigued by the caves and walked toward them. I saw a small wisp of smoke rise from behind the last dune, and heard the Ava Maria whispered in Spanish. I crouched in the reeds and moved very slowly.

When I was about ten yards from the small votive candle that sputtered and hissed before a terra cotta statue of the Virgin, I saw a young girl of about thirteen kneeling with her arms outspread and her neck craning up in what seemed an impossible position to hold for more than a few seconds. I remained hidden in the reeds.

She was about five and a half feet tall and had long black hair that fell to her waist. She wore bluejeans, a green windbreaker, and sneakers. Her face, as it caught the sunlight, was beautiful in its innocence and radiant in what seemed reflected light. She seemed unaware of her surroundings and the beach was deserted, so I knelt in the sand and waited. There was a shallow cave, like

102

a small grotto, a few yards above the sand where Guadalupe had her shrine. In this grotto, swallows were building nests. They wheeled and turned in their dance as they brought mud back to shore up the walls of their houses. I looked toward the ocean and listened to the waves crash for a long time. The fog had come in again and yet it was thin enough that light still played on the waves. The color moved from steel gray to blue to translucent green as a wave rose and broke, and then white as it spent itself on the beach. When I looked back at Guadalupe, she had fallen on her side. I felt a strange sense of calm and I thought I could almost hear whispers coming from the grotto. I went to her and knelt beside her. I could see her eyelids fluttering and her eyes moving rapidly side to side as they do during a dream. Slowly her body relaxed and her muscles twitched involuntarily.

Her hands were uncommonly cold and her breath came from deep within her in long waves. There was no wind and it was warm and sheltered where we were. Swallows danced overhead and waves broke like promises against the shore. The sands murmured a sibilant message and I felt blessed and found myself praying with something like devotion and understanding. *Ave Maria, gratia plena* . . . I must have been saying it out loud when Guadalupe awoke from her trance. She looked at me silently, her beautiful eyes full of light and sorrow, but not surprise.

"Why are you crying?" she asked.

"I don't know, it's been a long time since I've prayed."

"But you are a priest."

"Yes."

She was sitting now toying with the sand.

"Can you tell me," I said, "can you describe to me what you saw?"

"The other priest told me it was a sin to tell anyone."

"It is not a sin to tell me. It is not a sin to speak of it."

"I am afraid."

"Afraid of what? Of sin?"

She laughed, a girlish, adolescent laugh. "No, not of sin. I am afraid of the priests and all the people. I am afraid of what they will do to my family."

"You are not afraid of what you have seen?"

She laughed again, "Of course not, Father. Mary is very kind. She tells me not to be afraid, that she loves me." Her eyes filled with sorrow. "Our Lady is the only one who does not criticize or blame me."

"Who blames you?"

"Life is good here, better than in Mexico, but only if you are quiet. All the people are like hornets. My brothers do not want to lose their jobs. My mother thinks . . . something is wrong with me. That I make her life harder. The Virgin smiles, only smiles. She makes me feel good. She understands."

"Understands what?"

"About love, Father."

She stood and started up the beach toward a steep path up the cliff. I followed her. "No, Father. It is a long walk. You will not reveal my secret?"

"No."

"*Gracias.*"

"When will you come back here?"

"Friday."

"Can I speak to you again?" She shrugged and started up the trail.

I walked back up the beach, found the path and made my way slowly back to the car. I looked toward the cliff but it was deserted. I drove back to the inn and sat looking out the window until hunger forced me to move. I drove to town, to a restaurant called the Station House. The food was passable and the beer cold. I looked out the window and brooded. There was no doubt that Guadalupe was sincere. I had seen case studies and photographs of other apparition recipients and hers was consistent with the Beauraing and Garabandal episodes. Her desire for secrecy seemed sincere and her trancelike state genuine. It was clear she had nothing to gain except trouble from her experience.

Two women sat at a table near me. They spoke with a self-confident intimacy which so many American women have learned and men don't know enough to envy.

". . . But did you see Jean's face when we said the rosary?"

Their voices trailed off and I stopped listening. I went home and, after being subjected to a catalogue of maladies by the owner of the inn, went to bed and fell into a dreamless sleep.

CHAPTER
TWENTY-ONE

It is cold and dark where I write these words. Forgotten by God, exiled in time, hunted relentlessly by remorse, by the memory of passion, by more corporeal enemies. Only animal senses do I allow myself. I know when to fear, when to hide, how to leave no trail, or how to cross the trail over and over so as to create a labyrinth to confuse the hunter. I am the son of the fox with the scent of the dogs carried by every wind. And yet there are moments of remembered passion, moments at once mystical and profoundly profane. Memory which is only the battered citadel of time. Memory, that pool of fire in which I immerse myself to avoid the living flames of the present.

I meditate and meditate. Worlds move through me celebrating their living nature. My heart will open momentarily and I will see a small part of the truth with exquisite clarity. Then I am once more plunged into the dark river of my life and my mind once more races about in search of shelter, in search of food, in search of warmth, and yes, in search of sex. In a state of meditation, what the fathers called grace and everyone misunderstood, I can see in myself the life of an animal obeying the laws of its nature. Yet a part of my mind still criticizes into complete numbness every hopeful aspiration. I drag this personality around like a trunk that gets heavier the more I try to leave it behind.

I preach only as part of a magical charm against the death of forgetfulness, fearful that my story will remain untold. I preach to the empty church of the Word. I assure you I am considered mad by everyone who comes in contact with me. In the midst of flowers, in the midst of the unread entrails of birds, in the midst of a living cornucopia of haggling, I stand mumbling my rude charms and prayers at the foot of Bruno's statue. The drunks and addicts nodding off around the statue's base, like Pietàs lacking a compassionate mother, accept me as one of their own. My pilgrimage has become so regular that shopkeepers along my route set their clocks by my hurried passing, my cassock flying out behind me, my lips moving in prayer. The wheel of fortune has eradicated my name from every document that ever held it. If you want proof of my birth, of my first communion, of my confirmation as a soldier of Christ, of my deaconate, of my ordination, of my teaching assignments, you would find blank pages.

I hide unseen among them. I am invisible. My invisibility is the result of charms, heavenly and infernal, learned at the feet of Bruno's Egyptian tutors.

Rumor has it that Gabriel the Apostate has been sighted in Bangkok, in Chaing Mai, that he barely escaped from Lima, from Brasilia, from Buenos Aires. In truth I labor under their noses, cataloguing forbidden books in a secret library. I read and reread ancient Egyptian texts, laboriously translated by some forgotten cleric in the Middle Ages. I read again my beloved Beguines. With rage do I pull from the immense stacks the Inquisitional records on Bruno, Savonarola, Joan of Arc. My fingers tremble over the endless files on Lourdes, Fatima, Beauraing, Garabandal, Cairo, Madjugorie, Guadalupe, and even Point Reyes. The mystery grows and I wish only to complete this record, to synthesize the meaning behind her messages, her warning to the world, which has so little time to hear it and change.

CHAPTER
TWENTY-TWO

It took me over a week to get an interview with Jean. I left message after message on the answering machine at her office. Finally she agreed to talk with me.

"Do you know who I am?" I began. The afternoon was unraveling like a cheap carpet. I was irritated at being kept waiting, and my voice betrayed my chagrin.

"Yes," Jean said with a bitter laugh, "you're the ghostly bishop who haunts the shrine and takes longs walks on the beach. Never talk to anyone, just always there." I had heard her name every time the shrine on the cliffside was mentioned. Jean. Only one name seemed to be needed. She was a psychic and, rumor had it, a healer. Her gaze was full of interest and she seemed amused by my awkwardness. The intensity of her interest unnerved me. There was no convention to her beauty. There was too much strength in her features and her body had a martial quality, infused with the seriousness of her intention. There was no invitation to her beauty. It was elemental, natural and unadorned, like a spirit etched in color by Blake.

"But I've been trying for a week to arrange this talk with you," I said as she gestured for me to sit.

"And it makes me uneasy, I can tell you. You want to figure me out, shrink me down to manageable size."

"What *is* your interest in the Point Reyes apparition?"

"Isn't it obvious? Who wouldn't be interested? Let me tell you something. I know you don't believe in psychics—Jesus, you don't even believe in Roman

Catholic mysticism—so you're not going to listen. But Mary has been directing my life for a long time."

"Then you've seen her?"

"Listen, I'm not going to fit into your misconception. Is it more important to see her or to understand her message?"

"Then you haven't seen her, haven't had a real apparition?"

"Can I make you some tea? Some hear her, some feel her presence, some of us just *know*. Don't get tied to the program. You gotta, like, see her, touch the hem of her cloak, see her with the Christ child. I mean that's fine, but that's not what I'm talking about. I'm sure you've been told already I'm not Catholic, so Mary isn't part of that cultural thing for me. I was never voted Queen of the May in grade school, you know, Sodality of Mary, all that stuff. But I know her, you know what I mean?"

"I confess I don't know what you mean." I looked around. It was not the office of a therapist, there were oriental carpets and a large painting on the wall that seemed to draw the viewer through a mystic center into an unknown world.

"I know you don't. Cream or sugar? And I can't explain. All those old guys in Church history, one time or another, making pronouncements about Mary: Immaculate Conception, Virgin Birth, whatever. First of all they were guys. No disrespect, but they didn't have a clue to Mary except what made their agenda nice and tidy. You know, only a guy would think of the Virgin Birth and all that overshadowing business. Anyway, what's the deal? Had to make it, sex I mean, something bad, make the rest of us who get pregnant the old-fashioned way guilty, impure. Virgin Birth, come on! Mary doesn't care, thinks it's all a laugh, these guys making themselves feel better about not getting any. Saint Paul. Augustine. Bunch of guys. Sorry, but you've got to admit I'm right."

"And Mary, Mary tells you this?"

"It's all obvious anyway, isn't it? Mary talks to me about the heart. How to open the heart. Once you understand that, everything is different. Just that one thing. I can see that worries you."

"I'm just having trouble understanding you. You don't see her. She doesn't appear to you, not as a vision, or even a disembodied entity. There's no spatial or temporal shift, no trancelike state, no auditory experience. You admit to having no religious ties, no belief in the Church's tradition regarding Mary, no belief in the larger Christian body of belief, in short, no faith, and you wish me to believe that you have a very personal relationship with her, that she directs your life and speaks to you or causes you to know how to open your heart, and that you share jokes with her about the chauvinism of more than a thousand years of Church tradition?"

"Mary is cool, what can I say? You think there is a ticket or a password that allows you access and no one else? It just isn't so. You make all these divisions, make all these borders that separate everyone. The saved and the damned. Only a bunch of celibate men can tell the rest how to think. Then you set up some test to judge whether or not it's a miracle. I'm not claiming to be a saint, I'm no Bernadette, but my way of talking to her is as direct and simple as rain. At the same time it doesn't exactly depend on a belief that Rome got the record straight and that the Mary that Guadalupe sees and the Mary who speaks to me is the historical Mary that is such a meek pawn in the Gospels, which aren't exactly historical records anyway, right? More tea?"

"Yes. Thank you."

CHAPTER
TWENTY-THREE

"I don't like titles, they get in the way, like uniforms, don't you think? I'll call you Gabriel. Nice and proper. OK?" I had wanted to speak with Jean again, after our disastrous first meeting. This time, however, I chose the neutral ground of the Station House Cafe. "By the way," she continued, "I saw you the other day. You know, something about you doesn't fit at all. I saw you on the beach and you were pacing. Back and forth, back and forth like a caged animal. Then I see you close up and it's like you're so perfect, so controlled you're not there at all. What do you want from all this? You snoop around talking to people, asking questions like God's private eye with God only knows what agenda, I don't like to even think what it must be. Then I see you on the beach and I realize you're hiding something. Then I realize you're hiding everything."

I moved the plate in front of me a quarter of an inch. Then the silverware. I squared the edges of the napkin. I had tried to be more friendly, avuncular, and was meeting with absolutely no success. "Hiding everything is my job. It's my vocation, my talent."

"When someone hides everything, Gabriel, you wonder what they're hiding. Most people are an open book. Want something they don't have, have too much and can't give it away. Sex, food, work. Can't get started, finish too soon, can't finish at all. But the inside and the outside usually fit. Most of us have been pushed around, abused, abandoned. And we all try to hide the scars a little bit, but to anyone with a little intuition, it's right there."

"But not with me?" I was suddenly on the defensive and sweat was melting the starch in my collar.

"Not with you, Gabriel. You look like Houdini before they lower him into the water, all thick iron chains and gleaming locks. What I have to tell you is, be careful. The apparition changes everything, everyone who comes in close contact. You're here for a reason, a reason I see even if I don't understand. The Church doesn't have a clue to what's going on here, and when it finds out, it won't be happy. And I know the Church will try to say that what Mary's really saying is about sin, personal sin, and the need for even greater repression, and, excuse me, but that's a lot of shit.

"What Mary is saying is that we have to open our hearts. That sounds simple; but, like, what's an open heart supposed to be? Look around at the mess we've made of things. Could this have been done by people with open hearts? Well, it couldn't. It's all obvious, and it's obvious why you're here. What I'm saying is, you're in deep trouble and maybe you know it and maybe you don't. We're in the middle of something special, unrepeatable, a touch of the infinite. I've been in this game a long time, I've waited my turn, and this is it. It's not an aberration, it's not a hoax, it's not a dangerous example of mass hysteria. Mary is drawn here by our collective need and she voices our fears and longings. And we had better listen to her warnings and change. The environmentalists say we're going to destroy the planet, but they're wrong, the planet is just another rock. It might take a long time but it will survive. What we are doing is killing each other."

CHAPTER
TWENTY-FOUR

Life seemed to tumble down a soft hillside into a routine. The apparitions continued, but only Guadalupe and I knew when and where. I often met her at the small shrine beneath the cave and I would sit in meditation while her visions took place. Then we would talk for a while and take our separate paths home. My meditations brought me no closer to seeing or hearing the Virgin, yet I began to have an unshakable belief in Guadalupe and in the reality of her visions.

Fewer and fewer people visited the shrine on the cliff until only a devout group of twenty was left. The Giaquintos went about their business, the parish continued its quiet and smoldering schism, lacking only a new catalyst to ignite fresh disputes.

Jean and I met for tea or took long walks more and more often. At first I just wanted information, then I wanted to understand her position, and finally I wanted to understand myself. Soon the proprietor of the Estero tired of her complaints, and the parish priests tired of their suspicions. The other denizens of the community began to behave as though I were a slightly sinister shore bird lost and stranded during a migratory flight. I can think of no rational reason why I extended my investigation. It was as though I were held motionless to accommodate the turns and twists of fortune. It was like being held under water, everything slowing down, reduced to a slow motion of startling clarity.

In a dream one night I held a crystal globe above my

head. It became heavier and heavier until it required all my strength just to hold it. I awoke exhausted, nearly paralyzed with foreboding.

The next day it shattered.

CHAPTER TWENTY-FIVE

"Gabriel, I must see you. Something extraordinary has happened. I've been feeling Mary particularly close the last few days. So yesterday some friends, well, clients really, came up from L.A. They brought a woman I have been giving readings to for years. I mean she's been slipping deeper and deeper into her multiple personalities for years. Severely abused as a kid, held it together, became a musician, then about ten years ago memories of the abuse surfaced and she became aware of the multiples. Four then five.

"So Annie brings Serena to see me. We've all become friends. I know all of the personalities, and they sort of trust me. I suggest we take a walk on the beach. So we go out to Kehoe. This personality of Serena's comes right out, this fifteen-year-old girl, this real sexy ingenue, Serena calls her Kate and she is something. Willful as all get-out. Well, she marches right up to this spot below a cave, where starlings are building nests. A hundred of them are bringing mud and whatever to the cave and then flying back out. Very dramatic."

"Jean, Jean, hold on. I'll pick you up in a few minutes." I raced out, picked Jean up, and a half hour later we were walking up the beach toward a place I thought only Guadalupe and I knew about.

"Here it is." It was the place where Guadalupe had her apparitions.

"OK. Tell me what happened."

"Well, Gabriel, it was the most amazing thing. This personality, Kate, rushes up here like she's been here before. In a flash, just as we catch up with her, she finds a small statue hidden behind a rock. She puts it on the rock, making an altar of it. Now this Kate has always been wild, like perverse, always acting out, taking her clothes off in public, shoplifting designer clothes, coming on to all these older guys, you name it. Well, there we find her kneeling in prayer. I swear she is surrounded, surrounded, by this light and looks the very picture of innocence. Which, let me tell you is a stretch.

"Gabriel, why are you pale? Anyway, then Kate brings out Willie, this street-smart punk from the projects. Always protects Serena when she's in a dangerous situation. Willie will fight anyone. So here is Willie, and this is miraculous. Here is Willie with this silly smirk on his face kneeling in front of the statue. And then Willie starts to cry and brings out Serena One, a very adult version of Serena, but openly gay. Serena One kneels there smiling this beatific smile of pure energy and spirit and brings out Serena Two, the personality that kind of manages everything, the one that knows about the others and takes care of them, kind of a mother, really.

" 'There,' she says, 'that's the lot,' and falls into a dead faint in front of the statue. Gabriel, it was fantastic. She came to in a minute and she just lay there for a long time. Then she stood up and said, 'They're gone,' and she began to weep and cried for a long time. I mean, she knew then that she would have to face the feelings, deal with her memories of the abuse alone without a phalanx of personalities to help. She realized it was a mixed blessing at best, but a blessing nonetheless."

"It was Guadalupe's second shrine Serena found."

"It was your little secret. You are always one secret up, aren't you?"

"She, Guadalupe, I mean, has walked five or six miles to that spot every Friday since I've been here. Sometimes I meet her there and pray with her. Sometimes she wants to be alone. She is afraid of others finding out, of all the meanness and divisiveness that results from anyone knowing. She's, well, fragile."

"Oh, Jesus! It couldn't be helped, Gabriel. That spot glowed, at least to Serena. Whatever you think, these things get called up and they can't get stuffed back in, they don't fit anymore. And we need to know. We need to know, Gabriel."

"We don't need a circus," I said. "We don't need Guadalupe forced to endure the cameras, the mean questions, the wrath of her family. What is Guadalupe's should remain Guadalupe's. It belongs to her alone."

"Oh, no you don't. Something is happening, and not just to Guadalupe. To you and me, to all of us. You must see that Guadalupe, if she is strong enough to bear the vision, is strong enough to bear the result. She is the messenger. And she must bear witness."

"Jean, please, if word gets out, the message will be twisted by the media until it will no longer be Mary's or Guadalupe's. It will be usurped, deliberately misunderstood."

Jean's eyes dilated with anger and her voice rose over the sound of the pounding surf. "Don't you see? There are some who have prepared themselves to hear, who know what this means. They need to know so they can continue to change their lives, so they can influence others. If we hear the message, perhaps we can stop the madness before it's too late."

"Excuse me, but that's not likely. Once it gets out, whatever is real in this will be lost. It's my job to make sure the Church is not damaged and I've been doing it."

"Well, your job just got tougher. Tomorrow morning there's a procession to the shrine at the beach and for all I know the networks will have a satellite hookup by then. A miracle changes the game, you know."

"You've no idea, Jean," I was shouting by now, "no idea at all. Secrets are better kept, safer. This will destroy more than it will heal. Serena's experience, no matter how moving, would never be considered a legitimate miracle. A psychological breakthrough, yes, but those are not uncommon."

"Gabriel," Jean shouted back, "who are you trying to convince? I don't give a damn if some Vatican lackey gives his stamp of approval to this. Serena has undergone a profound experience, a healing. It took place in front of a shrine to Mary. That is enough for me. What are your motives here, anyway? Why were you really sent? To protect the Church's interests by strangling Mary's message before it could be heard? Well, get out of the way, Gabriel, because you're too late. After tomorrow the world will know and we will do everything in our power to make sure the right message comes through loud and clear."

"Please wait a few days. Let me talk to Guadalupe. Let me try to keep the media at bay. I have the power."

"Gabriel, I've got to get back. I can't, won't, stop now. You better get out of the way, this isn't Rome. Rome is a joke here. And the power of your high holy office won't silence us."

CHAPTER
TWENTY-SIX

She turned and walked away. I watched her slender form recede and leave me to the sound of surf and the call of the sea birds. I was not angry. A small tight twisted smile pulled at my lips. The wheel of fortune!

I knelt at the shrine and let my thoughts pound themselves to nothing in the sound of the ocean. I tried to open my heart, to hear Mary's message. I could hear what sounded to be murmurs through a wall too thick to allow words to pass. I was overwhelmed by the knowledge that events would occur in a pattern that I could not control. Behind the dread was acceptance, behind the peace was the knowledge that my life could never be the same. Once again I was listening to Father Dunstan.

Think of it, Gabriel. Innumerable worlds alive as we are alive. That's what Bruno saw. All connected in the striving to bear witness somehow to that aliveness. Innumerable worlds of infinite mystery, of infinite possibility, not the work of a superior intelligence but all of one fabric, space and time and whatever they consist of, all of it a shimmering immense dance that is God. Animated and peopled and alive. Bruno was inspired by magic, by the idea that all religion, all experience, was connected by a magical bridge and then Bruno just took off into the modern universe, not into our concept of the universe, but into a magical universe where all possibilities are contained. We are just reattaining his view, after all. That contemplation of the aliveness of the planets and stars must spur us on to change the way we inhabit this world. Magic led

Bruno straight to political revolution, and the mixture of the two led him to the stake.

I don't want to remember the next few days. They were hideous, filled with the terrors of video cameras, journalists, gawkers, and genuine pilgrims. A half-dozen people with a variety of ailments were either cured or went into spontaneous remission. I experienced each "miracle" as a personal blow. I was interviewed at length and repeated over and over the reasoned and sanitized version of the events. I leaned on the conservative approach so hard I could see the news analysts and anchor people wince and smirk as they went about their business.

There were candlelight processions and all-night vigils. Cheap statues of the Virgin were sold at roadside stands, cheaply printed pamphlets appeared giving fabricated transcripts of Mary's utterances that put the most conservative and homophobic words into her mouth. I worked ceaselessly at damage control, at containment. I tried and failed at every turn. The road to the shore was choked with recreational vehicles and the huge vans of the film crews.

Jean, for her part, attempted to tell her story, to give Mary's message to whoever would listen. She was interviewed by leering reporters who invariably found ways to dismiss her statements as nonsense. She became more strident, which only exacerbated the problem. Soon the media tired of her also and turned to Guadalupe, who only looked down with impenetrable melancholy.

After a week of this, I retreated into my bungalow with a bottle of scotch. My superiors had been trying to reach me and I didn't have the courage to return their calls or answer their cables. Instead I wrote long letters to Poncarelli and to Dunstan.

I stayed in the next day and the day after. I seemed to move as though underwater, my thoughts gliding by, detached and aimless like brightly colored fish. At about eleven, when the weariness and alcohol had dissolved the rhythmic pounding in my temples, I heard a knock at my door. I was sitting in an armchair in a dark room and didn't at first move to answer. The knocking was tentative but persistent. Finally I answered and found Jean, who said nothing but marched into the room and turned on the small lamp next to the chair.

"Took you long enough, Gabriel." I got another glass and poured two drinks.

"I don't drink," she said, taking the glass and draining it. I poured another. "Used to." She sat down and put her head in her hands. There was only one chair, so I genuflected next to her. She was wearing a long black skirt, a pullover sweater, and a handwoven Guatemalan shawl. Her face was streaked with tears.

I put my hand on her arm.

"I owe you an apology which you're not going to get," she said. "Everyone has been a beast, starting with you, and I don't feel like apologizing to anyone. Ever. You were right except you were wrong. Oh damn, damn, damn." She looked up at me with a fierce, angry glare.

"I tried so hard. I tried to be clear, but they made a fool of me. The whole town is a hostile shit pile, people buying Kmart madonnas and throwing the wrapping in the street. It's all my fault. I thought this time it would be different, but it's not and now it's a disaster. The place will never be the same. Goddamn right-wing Jesuits making Mary sound like goddamn Bishop Sheen. And you sounding so slick and reasonable, trying to say it's all some kind of mass hysterical reaction that will disappear tomorrow. Sanctimonious shit-heel." I poured us more scotch.

"I'm drunk for the first time in ten years," she said, "and that's your fault too. Where the hell have you been? Haven't the hell been out on the barricades."

"Licking my wounds."

"That's a full-time job if I ever saw one."

"I did what I could. In front of the camera, behind the scenes. I blackmailed. I threatened. This thing just took on its own life. And, frankly, my heart wasn't in it. But you were great. I mean it. Clear, courageous, you didn't swear at their rudeness and didn't use too much New Age cant." Jean looked at me and her gaze softened to only mild misanthropy.

"You're not a real bishop."

"No."

"Any more surprises?"

"Can't think of any at the moment."

"Are you as self-contained as you act?"

"No one is as self-contained as I act."

"Well, you're pretty convincing."

"It's not an act."

"It's also not that convincing. Anyone with an ounce of intuition can see through you in a minute."

"How long did it take you?"

"Half a minute. I'm a pro." Then she leaned over and kissed me. Everything happened so fast and yet seemed to take place in slow motion. The long kiss tasting of whiskey and tears, the long kiss with Jean kissing me, like a woman leading a man in a slow dance. It wasn't what I ever imagined it would be, her tenderness leading me through seemingly endless rooms crowded with the unused furniture of loneliness, until at the end I was naked and not alone. I tried to hold on to each new sensation, to the astonishing beauty of her breasts as she brought my head down to kiss each nipple, leading again, guiding me through the awkwardness until I was naked also of my nakedness, guiding my hands and my kisses to belly and thighs. I tried to remember, to savor, but there was the onrushing, the breath of her, the arching of her back, until she stopped my kisses and lay back with her knees raised and guided my cock into her and then I was over her, supported by my arms because I also wanted to watch and there was a look of reproof and almost a smile as she reached up and drew me down and then slipped her arms around my back to embrace me as I thrust into her with no other thought, no other intention, until there was, finally, no one left to manage the remembering, the ordering of experience, no one left to be shocked by the unprecedented, blinding sensations, except a naked man joined to a woman in an act of love that could be recalled but never remembered.

"What are you smiling about? Proud of yourself or what?"

"No, not proud."

"You're not going to start feeling guilty, are you?"

"I promise. It's just—"

"Listen, it's been a while for me, too."

"I didn't realize . . . I mean, my inhibitions have always been like housebroken pets."

"Maybe it's like they say, inhibitions are soluble in alcohol."

"No, it's not that. I must confess I've been drawn to you from that first day."

"That old black magic. It's simple, I'm a witch."

"What now?"

"Well, let's see. Maybe we both have some catching up to do."

Perhaps it was witchcraft and I fell under a spell. We talked and made love. I remember the moonlight on her skin, remember waking early in the morning with her thigh thrown over my legs, with the taste of her like a sacramental, and the smell of her like incense. I had taken leave of my senses—no, I had taken leave of everything *except* my senses. In the brief periods of sleep that punctuated our lovemaking, I dreamed that I dried the tears of the weeping Madonna, that I danced a mad erotic dance in the midst of a dazzling circle of grain and then the grain was on fire and I was on fire and there was no beast to carry me away.

We awoke finally, pierced by the sunlight of a rare clear morning. I came back to myself, startled and transfixed by our nakedness. Jean looked at me with amusement. "You OK, Gabriel?"

"I feel a little naked, like Adam, aware of it for the first time."

"Well, don't expect me to offer you an apple. It's the

sexiest part of the Bible, don't you think, I mean that part about Eve and her seed and crushing the head of the snake? Very sexy." As she spoke, she traced the intricate coils of a snake on my body. "I mean, I always root for the snake. Knowledge of good and evil, why the hell not. Five or ten minutes, you're bored with paradise already. Hosanna this, hosanna that."

"Temptress."

"Somebody's got to do it or nothing happens. Sinning is knowledge, look at it that way. You could use a tattoo or two, you know. You don't have enough scars. Scars are the history of sin, the library of all knowledge. Oh, here's one. Well, like, a small scar is better than none."

"You are a witch and I'm a fallen priest."

"Not a moment too soon or a softer place to fall."

And she clung to me fiercely, as one pursued, as one hounded into the consummation of the moment. I was the precipice she clawed at for safety. And I returned her embrace with equal violence. I burned with longing that seemed to reach back beyond me into the lives of all the lonely and they inhabited me with their urges as the sea is urged toward shore, is forced almost against its will to arch its back, to curl, to hurtle toward release, toward that moment of absorption before being separated once more into the salt-heavy ocean.

CHAPTER
TWENTY-SEVEN

I was awakened midmorning by a loud knocking. I
threw on trousers and shirt and answered. It was the
owner of the inn, with an express package. "I signed for
this." She was wearing sunglasses, but I could see that
she was doing her best to look past me into the room.
I wanted to laugh, but just nodded in response and
closed the door. I went back to the bedroom and sat on
the edge of the bed. I tore open the cardboard wrapper and found a thick envelope with the seal of the
Vatican.

> Excellency,
>
> We are accustomed to receiving answers to our
> urgent messages and cables. As you must be
> aware, the measures you have taken have met
> with little success. Events threaten to over
> whelm the paltry defenses you have raised. You
> are to continue your efforts until you receive
> further instructions. You will then be given a sig
> nal after the reception of which you must leave
> Point Reyes secretly and return by an indirect
> route to Rome. Do not make contact or impede
> our actions in any way.
>
> Signorelli

I could see the bald, featureless face impassively ordering my demise, and I shivered as though I could hear
the wheel of fortune spinning like a roulette wheel.

Jean came out of the bathroom, drying her hair. "I heard a knock."

"The landlady with a sinister package from my superiors and what will become vicious, if supportable, rumors concerning us."

"She certainly doesn't miss much."

"I think she is dialing already."

"Gabriel, I'm sorry."

"Good God, don't be. My real worries begin in Rome. I can't imagine what is going through their minds, but I would much rather be their agent than their target."

"I tried to warn you, remember?"

"I remember."

"What are you going to do?"

"Put on some very strong coffee, take a shower, and pray for a natural catastrophe."

"Good plan. I'll make the coffee."

We had a few cups of coffee and talked as intimate and lifelong friends talk, making inconsequentials into deep and involving conversation layered with hidden meaning and unspoken promises. At ten o'clock she slipped out as decorously as possible and I commenced pacing until I had worn through my thoughts. Then I drove to the beach, past a town that was suffering an invasion, in a long line of cars heading toward the miraculous. I abandoned my car a mile down the road and walked the rest of the way. Any hopes of the fresh sea breezes clearing my head quickly vanished. The air was charged with expectations, with the desperate need for novelty that exists at the gates of rock concerts, football games, and peep shows.

There was a crowd of about two thousand milling about on the beach, hoping for an apparition, a spectacular cure, or an unmistakable sign from heaven. A bank of fog hung over the water like a shroud and soon enveloped the beach and grotto in its mists. A few small fires fought with the wind and lost. Just south of the grotto, someone had erected a tent to shelter the crippled and sick who had been carried to the beach on stretchers or on chairs.

On the cliff overlooking the grotto, I thought I saw Guadalupe, who stood for a moment and then disappeared. I moved off down the beach in the other direction and I walked for a long time until I was sure I was alone. Then I found a place among the reeds where I would be hidden, sat in the sand, and tried to think of nothing at all.

CHAPTER
TWENTY-EIGHT

"You don't know what it's like, having multiples."

"I would like to understand."

Serena was about forty-five, and although she wore a look of seriousness, her features tended to blur and then recompose themselves. Her body seemed always a little out of focus, its contours masked by oversize shirts and slacks. She wore her hair short and slicked down against her head.

"I don't know, maybe you can, Jean says you're all right. It's not what you think. Ever since that day on the beach, when I stumbled on Mary's grotto, I haven't had the multiples and it scares me."

"I would imagine you would be relieved."

"See, that's what people think. They only see what they call sickness and think I should feel grateful to be well, but it's not that easy. I had four multiples, all distinct, all with their own function, their own agenda. This person who is talking to you now is new. I call her Serena, but I don't know her exactly. I don't mean that. It's hard, you see, because if Serena is talking to you, who is the 'I' that is aware of her? You see the problem?

"One of us was Willie, this tough guy about eighteen. Nobody messed with him. He was ready for anything, ready to kill. I lived on the streets for a while and Willie was there most of the time. Macho, a little paranoid, a regular guy. I lived in the park, in the city, and there was danger all the time. Other street people, punks, cops, and social workers, they all wanted to mess with you. But not with Will. Serena, who was just part of the action then, started to be aware of him. And they had to work it out. I mean Serena was a real dyke, hated men, wouldn't give 'em the time of day, and there's Willie, this tough guy, very macho, you know what I mean? So they had to get to know each other, talk it out. Serena got to accept him, even to like him. Willie, well, he was too cool, but he was coming around. Serena who is now the 'I' who is talking to you, the one who is left, misses him. And who is going to protect her? Maybe she is tough, too, I don't know.

"When I came upon that statue of Mary, I went into a kind of trance. Suddenly all the parts of me decided to integrate, and Serena seemed the strongest, and she was the one who carried the banner for the others. Miraculously, you might say, I was changed. I didn't actually see her, understand, not a vision, but a power, a presence of something, someone strong enough to upset the balance.

"And, well listen, I'm not complaining but all I'm left with is a personality alone in the world. One personality seems a little restrictive, like a tight pair of shoes to someone who grew up barefoot. I am uncharted territory. I think I am on the way to real integration, although I'm convinced that doesn't happen to very many people. Maybe because I'm starting off from a position of *dis*integration, I'll know wholeness when I see it."

"Do you think most people aren't integrated?"

"They aren't, that's all. They have a weak structure to hang all their different voices on. My abuse was serious enough that the organizing self had to give up, distribute the pain around, and let each find a way to live with a little of it. I survived. Now maybe it's time that the fragments work together, maybe they can take the pain without splintering. But I know we all have voices held in check by a central self that organizes feelings and memories, and I know we shift among them all the time. We talk of personae, masks, very glibly, but never realize that they are as real as anything."

"Do you think Mary cured you?"

"To tell you the truth she didn't do me any favors. There was enough power in the event, enough *presence*, to pull me. There was power there, tremendous power. But I have to tell you, I don't know if I can pull it off."

"And you didn't see her or hear her speak?"

"What do you want me to say? You want me to let you off the hook? I don't even know what hook you're on. Maybe one of the multiples saw or heard, Serena didn't. But what difference does it make?"

CHAPTER
TWENTY-NINE

I scarcely believe I now am the same person who gave those interviews. I know now the pain of which Serena spoke. Voices become disembodied, cut off from the center. We are all a hall of voices, kept in tenuous check just one side of madness or the other.

Has the orderly voice disappeared?

It has not. But neither does it dominate.

Has this made me more healthy?

I know that, like Serena, each step toward integration is a step over red-hot coals, over broken glass. Like her, I know that I had constructed a voice that lessened the pain, that sheltered me from harm. It also sheltered me from experience, from delight in my own body, from the fullness of memory, from the possibilities of a future. It was order that constructed the wheel, and order that accepted too easily my place on it.

"Bishop, is it still your contention and the contention of your superiors that Guadalupe's grotto has *not* been the scene of miraculous or paranormal events?"

"The evidence is inconclusive at this time. There seem to have been spontaneous cures, if you will, but there are many explanations that fit the circumstances. Many maladies were psychogenic in nature and able to be affected by strong suggestion. We all know this to be true. There has been no report of mass experience, or other inexplicable phenomena such as occurred at Fatima and Lourdes. Even in those cases, few truly miraculous healings occurred and some investigators have called into question the mass experiences. There is precedent from other venues that suggests mass hallucination and hysteria as possibilities. The Church is charged with guarding its tradition and with being ever watchful that events don't run before reason and true faith."

"Will this episode be investigated further?"

"That is not in my hands."

"We understand there is a team on its way from Rome."

"I have nothing further to report, gentlemen and ladies, thank you."

CHAPTER
THIRTY

I dreamed that an osprey had caught a fish and was tearing pieces of it off and feeding it to its young. It sat on the railing of a small wooden pier that jutted out into the glassy water of the bay. It was beautiful, the calm water, the sun glinting off the silver body of the bird, which seemed almost gentle in its feeding ritual. I realized in the dream that it was behaving according to its nature and I awoke with the horrible realization that I was not.

CHAPTER
THIRTY-ONE

"You've stopped giving interviews," Jean said.

"It is useless."

"They're camped outside your door. What happens if they follow you here?"

"I am careful."

"But what happens?"

"I get burned at the stake."

"Not very funny."

"I understand it hurts like the very devil."

"No, really. What happens if they find out you're screwing the local *strega*?"

"Wet wood for sure."

"Be serious."

"They might be relieved it's not a local altar boy like so many of my brethren."

"You refuse to be serious."

"They might start looking into my background, trying to query my superiors."

"Who are your superiors?"

"I don't have any, at least not any they can query."

"That secret?"

"More secret than that."

"Then, as they say, your ass is out in the wind."

"Actually, it is under your blanket."

"Same thing."

"Not entirely."

It was a mile or two at the most from the inn to Jean's small A-frame house situated up a dirt road cul-de-sac. The reporters, and whoever else was watching, waited for me to either enter or exit from the inn. They would hound me for interviews, which with less and less civility, I refused to give. Then I would get into the car and drive away. Only a few followed. None of them expected me to step out of character, much less out of what they assumed to be my nature. They all, at least in the beginning, suspected me of little more than stubbornness and irritability. And, I say with a certain pride, none suspected that beneath my stern and diplomatic exterior beat the heart of a man.

This, of course, is at the heart of all disguises, at the heart of all personality, the expectation that it is a seamless whole, consistent in its needs and fulfillment. The assumption that to be one with our nature is to have tamed the warring voices, not to have given ourselves over to them. I had been taught to play with parts of my personality, in the Abruzzi, in England, and then in California, until the outer personality began to shift too easily and then to disappear, leaving me to the inner cacophony of voices.

My memories take on the aspect of feverish visions, the beauty of the *estero*, of the marshes, of the seashore mingled with my face in her hair, of the smell of her skin, of its glow after lovemaking. There were white kingfishers there, beautiful on the wing, soaring and gliding just over the water, and the pulling in of wings and the dive.

There were mornings so gray I could barely discern the water from the sky. Parts of my life have had that same quality, while inside there was the soar, the glide, and the dive.

Dear Gabriel,

By the time this letter finds you, I will have left this place and the priesthood. I began what I thought was a ministry years ago. I wanted to bear witness, to speak of life and the joy of God, and have ended being fit only for Extreme

Unction, for anointing the white and pitiful feet of the dying with a bit of oil. The people here have more of God than they need. I cannot bring them more or one of a different kind, I could only wish to bring them less, one less stern and unforgiving, but they would not understand or listen.

Do not think, Gabriel, that it is a crisis of faith, it is not. I can serve my God better at a distance than I can as his representative. And this has made me think of you, who seemed to bear that mantle so easily, and yet I think it is no more your nature than mine. And perhaps I hope you are struggling with this.

Tomorrow, I leave for Umbria where I have taken a job as a stonemason. Humble, but actually quite well paying.

I will be living near a small village called Niccone. If you have need of me, I will be there. Somehow our paths seem fated to cross.

I am sad that the Church of Rome is neither an old wine in a new skin nor a new wine in an old one. It finally feels empty to me, yet I find I am not empty. And with that exhilaration, I leave the black mantle behind me.

Yours,
Poncarelli

CHAPTER
THIRTY-TWO

"Gin and tonic tonight, Gabriel. It's too easy to be depressed when all you drink is scotch and brandy," Jean shouted from the kitchen. I paced uneasily around the small square of her living room. It was filled with books on goddesses, eastern religion, witchcraft. There was barely space for the shrines to various female deities and I shuddered slightly at the smell of unknown incense. I shrugged and smiled weakly to myself. She handed me a drink and caught my strange look.

"I forget," she said a little sadly. "This is all a little new to you."

"Nothing, nothing could have prepared me," I said, laughing. "I don't understand, I confess. My life has been spent following one rather narrow trail."

"Damn narrow, if you ask me. It was, like, all your saints and mystics lived in some magical time, and then it all ended in about the fourteenth century."

"But does your taste have to be so, well, pantheistic?"

"Ah Gabriel, I finally understand the term 'hermetically sealed.' Where were you when the world was changing, when we rediscovered Tibet and India? The goal was never orthodoxy. The goal, you know, was to get there, I mean *there*. Higher states, maybe just high, but we were serious. God knows what you were doing, nose in some text, probably on the same trail but didn't know it."

"I doubt it."

I followed Jean into the kitchen. She was making an

attempt at cooking polenta that made up in athleticism what it lacked in *contadina* patience. "Don't be so damn sure," she continued, punctuating her phrases with stirring flourishes. "That's what the mystics were all about. All that dancing at weird hours. All the wandering, all those troubadours, and the alchemists and magicians, all those poor dear witches and warlocks, all came down the same road. Higher states. So what were we doing? Some drugs, sure, acid for a while, mescaline, peyote, whatever. Your Beguines, we were like your Beguines with a little, you know, pharmacology thrown in."

I laughed.

"We were serious, goddamn it, Gabriel. We weren't just hippies. We wanted to see God and the way to see God was through the conscious mind, the ego. I mean, you had to get rid of it. The Sufis were hip, but who knew anything about Sufism in the sixties? About twenty very strange people in the Haight. Anyway who needs all that singing and dancing in strange robes when, like, there's acid. Drop a cap and you can fold the ego into small squares like an old Juicy Fruit wrapper.

"But, well, things got weird, as you can imagine. I mean no one had a fucking clue about what to do with these altered states once you got there. Our minds were so blown, who cared about God? A few of us crept off to nurse the acid flashes, and then started a whole round of meditation retreats, ashrams, tantric sex games, yoga, tarot. The goal was always to kill the ego in order to reach higher states. OK, we were fools. At least we were trying. You had a whole tradition behind you, a couple thousand years of visions and hermetic knowledge, and you didn't give a shit except to sell a few candles and build drafty churches.

"Tell me the truth. You think polenta is worth it? It's almost aerobic." Jean stirred furiously, intent, yet lost in her own thoughts.

"It was fun, cheap dope, jet-set maharishis, everyone going around stoned, refusing to tell you their mantra.

Our egos got soggy, smoked, twisted, got our brains fucked into mush, got taken for a long oriental ride, but the damn thing survived. We blasted it, seduced it, dressed it up in strange robes, but when the drugs wore off and the guru went off to the next stop on the book tour, there it was in the mirror taunting us.

"Stop looking so superior. It was a hell of a party. Somewhere along the line, I was going a little crazy— you know, guys who started out fine, a little weird on acid, going straight through the other stuff and ending up on heroin, which is like a coin-operated God. Dickheads.

Anyway I was on about the fourth addict and I was desperate. Went to a psychic. This woman, about forty, with long hair and strange eyes, this psychic, gave me a reading that blew my mind. All the teachers had sort of sneered at it, said it was an aberration, a dangerous side-track, but what did they know?

"So I said I don't give a damn, maybe it *is* a diversion, off the track, but this psychic business is at least an interesting diversion. For a few minutes, a few precious minutes, I'm out of this personality. For a little time there's only the client and the client's problems. I mean, isn't it just so, well, oppressive, carrying this personality around? No matter where you are, there is this voice that's supposed to be you yammering all the time. Who wouldn't want out once in a while, a real vacation.

"When I was younger I tried, I really tried, to get out of myself, do all this wild stuff, do things just because they were not me, but it was so disappointing, it all ended up to be me too. Like we have this great faculty for leveling our experience, making the extraordinary ordinary. Our personalities constantly whittle reality down to size until there is no spontaneity.

"Take all this Mary stuff. You were sent here to level it all, make sure nothing extraordinary happened, make sure the conscious mind got its daily dose of disappointment."

"Hey." I had finished my gin and tonic by that time. I found I was still thirsty. I made us both another drink.

"Well, it's true, Gabriel."

"The conscious mind was my employer."

"Sad but true. I realize talking about it, it's all the same thing. All my life I've been looking for a way out. A way out and a way in. In the psychic work I can get out for a few precious minutes each day, and I feel free, but then I gotta pick up the personality where I left off and it drives me nuts. Understand?"

"I'm beginning to."

"All these people come to me, failed by therapy, relationships, career, religion, you name it, and all they want is a little forgiveness, a moment's peace from the relentless voices of guilt and fear."

"Are you talking about me now?"

"Yeah, sure, I'm talking about you now. Where'd you get all this order crap anyhow? And look how you turn that need outward against people, people who need something as simple as a moment of transcendence, of forgiveness."

"It's the only structure I've ever known, the only reasonable existence I can think of."

"Gabriel, this stuff better be done, because I'm a little drunk and damn hungry."

The next day was gray, with a high fog over the ocean, a sky of soiled linen. In the afternoon, Jean and I rode out to the seashore to take a walk. We had been avoiding the grotto and the threats of media intrusion, but we somehow found ourselves skirting the marsh, found ourselves on its immense stretch of sand. It was cold and the beach was deserted except for two small figures I could barely discern in the distance. We wandered up the beach toward the grotto of Guadalupe's visitation. It, too, was deserted. We didn't speak as we walked; a languidness informed our every gesture, as though there were time for everything, as though there would always be time. I can't say why we stopped there or why we instinctively knelt in prayer in front of the small statue of Mary. Just as I can't tell you why my face felt suddenly flushed and then burning as if my skin were being scalded. Jean sensed something was odd and touched my hand. Her touch felt as though it came from a great distance and her fingertips were like ice. I looked up and the grotto was filled with light and I fell face down on the sand. I did not hear voices and wasn't told a secret prophecy of the future. I don't know how long I lay there. Somewhere in the distance, I heard Jean's voice calmer and more musical than any voice I had ever heard but I could not hear what she was saying. My soul was branded, seared with heat. There was no form to the light, no visage appeared out of it. But the message was clear and will never be lost to me.

. . . And would not be lost to thousands who soon saw the photograph of me, seeming to glow, which appeared coast to coast as soon as the photographer, one of the distant specks on a deserted beach, filed his photo, taken with a telephoto lens from at least five hundred yards away.

I cared little at the time. I came back to real sensations and real time about fifteen minutes later. I looked at Jean and her face was angelic although her expression was one of alarm and concern.

"God, you look beautiful," I said.

"What the hell is going on, Gabriel?"

"I seem to have had my own small apparition."

"Jesus."

"Closer to Mary."

"You saw her?"

"Not exactly."

"What then?"

"I'm supposed to ask the questions."

"Tell me, damn it."

"More felt her presence. I feel like something was burned from my soul and what is left is a sense of calm and . . . a little dread."

"Why dread?"

"I had to surrender something. I thought I could go back to the same life I lived before. Now I realize it's impossible."

"I could have told you that."

"You did. Isn't it nice to have your intuition confirmed by a higher authority?"

"I don't know . . ." Jean's voice and the sound of the ocean seemed to come from another world entirely. She was saying, "Well, why shouldn't you feel that way? Your old life stunk. Admit it. You were a shit, unlovable, uptight, snooty, you name it. Why would anybody want to go back to that?"

"It was safe."

"So is being dead."

"Why did you . . . why were you . . . ?"

"Most men—most men are too easy to read. Most men aren't well . . . damaged enough for me."

"I'm glad I fit into a valued category."

"Oh you do, believe me you do . . . I'm worried now you might change and I'll lose interest."

"You needn't worry."

"Are you OK, Gabriel? Can you, like, walk?"

"Never felt better."

"Then let's go back to my place."

The world seemed beautiful and innocent. I turned the frowning faces of Paul, Augustine, and Aquinas to the wall. There was no original sin and no reason to leave the garden.

After a few days, I left Jean's bed in the hours before dawn and returned to the Estero. I wandered about for a while and finally lay down on the bed and fell asleep. I slept so deeply I barely heard the telephone.

"Gabriel. It's Jean. Do you get a newspaper there?"

"Of course not."

"Well, you better get one. You made page three. Mystery cleric photographed at shrine with mystery woman. Juicy stuff, Gabriel."

I lifted a blind and saw a ring of newsmen and photographers waiting for me. With a silent groan that

142

stirred the depths of my soul, I showered, shaved, dressed, and ventured out to meet them.

"Bishop D'Amato, did you see the Virgin? The photograph clearly shows you in some kind of trance. Yet you have repeatedly debunked any mystical explanations and led us on with Vatican rhetoric. Bishop, please explain why no one at the legate's office has ever heard of you and Rome won't answer our calls?"

"Rome does not answer calls, as you must know. As for the photograph, I offer no explanation, none whatsoever. There are mysteries for which there are no explanations, and therefore it would be imprudent for me to offer one. Thank you."

From the back of the crowd I heard a voice I remembered, a voice that belonged to a reporter named Jonas Quigley. "Look," he shouted over the heads of the other reporters, "I've been trying for months to get you to say what's going on, get the Church's slant. You've been saying that nothing mystical is going on and then we see you splayed out in front of Mary's grotto. It won't work. My editors have been cabling Rome all night and they say they've never heard of you. More cables and still no records, not of your ordination, not even your confirmation or first communion. We need answers and you've been bullshitting, pardon me, for months. You have been carrying the Vatican's water and now they say you don't exist. Maybe they're embarrassed, you know, they don't like their priests making such good copy. What I mean is, maybe you should level with us, give us the real story. What have you got to lose?"

I retreated and fixed myself a cup of coffee with a stiff side of scotch. I paced. Every few minutes a reporter would lose his patience and knock loudly on the door. I shook with panic and with fury. The telephone kept ringing. When it stopped for a minute, I called Jean.

"Gabriel, it's terrible. They're camping in my front yard. I can't move. I'm paralyzed. They seem to be asking all the right questions. I don't know what to say. Gabriel, I'm scared."

"It's the same here. We've got to get rid of them. My superiors have conveniently destroyed all traces of me. I don't exist, no one can even prove I'm a priest."

"What are we going to do?"

"Pack a bag. I'll get rid of them somehow and meet you somewhere. Any ideas?"

"Yeah, wait a minute. A client of mine, rich guy, has a house on the ridge. He's gone, leaves a key in a pot next to the door. If we can get there, we're home free."

"If we can shake them, you mean. I'm not worried about the reporters. I worry about my former employers. They don't take kindly to such visible disasters. Give me the address and I'll meet you as soon as I can."

I put the phone down just as the door opened. The owner of the Estero was framed in the doorway.

"My roses. My herb garden. I have rare plants out there. Trampled. I can't have this. My liver is acting up. I'm breaking out in a rash. This could set me back months. *Months*. Do you know what this will cost me? Thousands. The noise. The fumes from their vans. They all smoke. This is killing me. I won't stand for it. Out. You have an hour." She turned and began to regale the reporters with a catalogue of her ailments. I took the opportunity to throw a few unclerical clothes, my half-empty bottle of scotch, and my notes into a cloth bag. I climbed out the bathroom window, which was at the rear of the house, and keeping the house between me and the small throng that was collecting around the front I made an ungainly and humiliating, but successful escape.

I walked about a mile off the road toward the bay along a bird watchers' path. I found a few trees that offered shelter and sat in the shade of one of them. I took stock of the situation. I was not dressed as a priest, but I had priest written all over me. Black tennis shoes and slacks, white shirt, cardigan sweater. My hands were shaking and I felt faint. I realized that returning for the car was out of the question. I was conspicuous and vulnerable. By now everyone in the community knew me. By now everyone on the whole continent knew me.

I got up slowly and walked along the path. Soon I was out of sight of the inn. A slight breeze blew through the trees. Gulls and an occasional pelican glided past me, their halcyon whiteness only serving to remind me of the desperateness of my situation.

The sun was high and my head was pounding. My thoughts far outraced the quickness of my steps. I remembered the compassion and sympathy I had felt. My bitter laugh at the brevity of those feelings woke me to my surroundings. The echo of that laugh follows me always, for it is the laughter that accompanies the wheel as it plunges toward despair. I did not know despair then, only that laugh which is its harbinger. It was Adam's laugh through a mouthful of apple, at the moment when intention becomes consequence. Had I not recognized it as mine alone, I would have said it was the laughter of the devil.

CHAPTER
THIRTY-THREE

"Gabriel, I can't tell you how happy I am to see you. But let me say one thing, you are a mess. Did you swim or crawl here? Did anyone see you? Oh sweet Jesus, what a mess. You are beautiful. I made a fire, found some canned soup, and listen, some great cognac. Come sit by the fire. If I weren't so scared I would think this was very exciting, well, sexy even. Don't you look a little crazed! Nothing like crashing through the woods with assholes at your heels to scrape that Roman arrogance away. Don't you miss those starched collars? Don't you miss the polite nods of the faithful? Oh, you're shivering. Nothing worse than being cold and wet, is there? I'll run you a hot bath. You know it is kind of sexy, even with the fear."

"You look a little more human."

"Marginally."

"No. Very attractive. Kind of caveman clerical. I like it, but I don't think it'll catch on. You like the place?"

"It's pleasantly remote. I'm beginning to love dead ends. You weren't followed?"

"I swear."

"Then we may be safe for a few hours."

"Gabriel. I don't, you know, like to pry, but who the hell are we running from? I mean I've never thought much of the Church, but I've never exactly thought of them as thugs."

"I'm not sure yet, exactly. I just know they, we, demand tidy appearances. They can't leave me roaming around talking to reporters after they've so carefully excised me from their rolls."

"Yeah, but come on. I'm pretty paranoid on a good day, but I never thought of them hiking up their robes and chasing anyone either."

"How much Church history do you know? The Vatican can hike up its robes and run with the best of them when it has to. Besides, they don't do their own running, their own hunting. It's more subtle. They have relationships with various organizations, reciprocal relationships."

"Well, I know about the Inquisition and the Middle Ages and burning witches and a few innocent bystanders. But it's ancient history, Gabriel. Isn't it?"

"Are you willing to bet your life it's ancient history? There's a fat bald monsignor who hasn't left the Vatican in thirty years who would like to think he is the heir of the Inquisition. Would like to think that what he does, he does for the good of the Church, which must be God's will. On a certain level, God's will transcends a few niceties."

"You're kind of scary sometimes, if you want to know the truth."

"I'm sorry I've brought you into this."

"I thought I brought *you* into it, so don't start acting so uppity. Maybe your heart opened a little. So you didn't do anything to me, OK?"

"Still, I don't understand you. You don't need me. I'm a liability. A failed priest, now a bad one, but—"

"I may be a little in love with you, if you have to know. You're a little slow in that department, Gabriel."

"Impossible. No one has ever been in love with me. I'm completely unlovable. I've raised unlovability to an art."

"Don't I know it. But that doesn't change anything. I've loved a lot of shits, a lot worse ones than you, lots worse. So don't hide behind your unlovability. Is that all you can say?"

"I'm sorry."

"You're not that sorry."

"This is impossible. I've never had these feelings, never wanted them, never longed for anyone, felt the need to touch, been desperate until I saw someone, needed a kiss, needed sex. Now I do and I'm not sure whether I gained or lost something. You stir passions, impulses in me that I always thought were alien to my nature. I always considered that my lack of feeling made me superior. Oh God, I'm blurting. This is terrible. I never confess."

"Gabriel, do you love me?"

"Yes."

"There. Was that so difficult?"

"Yes."

CHAPTER
THIRTY-FOUR

I learned the art of memory at the feet of Bruno. Elaborate meditations in which each memory becomes part of a room and each room part of the house of memory. A chamber of nightmares to rival any, yet with corners, niches of such sweetness. I search every room for those respites. Behind all is the sound of a heart beating without hope, beating faster as its inevitable end draws nearer. I have memorized those moments, that time. At night, instead of sleep, I take each day out of its niche and look at it, pore over it in search of a meaning to give my life.

It's all nonsense, giving life meaning, a small holdover from my days as a believer. I am obsessed with finding the pattern from which meaning derives, like an image forming from the bits of glass in a mosaic. I have lived and am about to die. I write this small treatise as a gravestone, nothing more. And yet memory is the manifestation of the pattern and these patterns are my only bequest. My life describes an arc of fate, a turn of the wheel.

At one time I would have fancied myself a reformer, trying with stirring sermons to affect the lives of those who hear. But I do not have the tireless optimism or the faith of the reformer. Did not Savonarola, Luther, Francis, Catherine, even Bruno push against the corrupt patrilineage and break themselves against it?

Since that time, fathers have begat fathers. Isn't that the strange meaning of celibacy? Do not proud animals vie with one another for the right to enter into the female mystery and participate in it? Is not their strength only added to the strength of women? How sterile then is the celibate who, like Paul, counts himself closer to God the Father by his refusal to participate in life's most precious dance, who recreates himself in sexless rites in which power passes from one old man to another?

Rome is beautiful this winter. The northeast wind blows cold and true. I hurry along the back streets desiring a few more days to finish this history, and set my house in order.

I sense them ever closer, I can almost smell their aftershave. Over and over, I walk every street in this labyrinth, note every alley, memorize every turn, until I am as comfortable as a wolf in an ancestral forest.

CHAPTER
THIRTY-FIVE

Jean refused to see the mark of a priest on me. In fact, she was fascinated by every aspect of the priesthood and treated me as though I came from an exotic culture with strange customs and rites with which she wanted to become accustomed.

"Tell me something, Gabriel. Didn't you ever fantasize about, you know, sex? Your most sexy years were sacrificed, weren't you ever just horny?"

"Never." It was the middle of the night. We had been awakened by the sound of a deer walking on the wooden planks of the porch. Our hearts raced with terror until we placed the sound. I got up and looked out the window. A stag with an elaborate rack of horns stood sniffing the air. He was illumined by the dull glow of a porch light which gave his exquisitely poised form a magical force. He looked once in my direction and disappeared into the woods that ringed the house. Jean laughed with relief as I returned to bed.

"It was just an omen. Come on, Gabriel, now you have to answer me. Hopefully no one else was watching. It's all a little ironic, but I guess we're making great strides. So tell me, I want to know everything."

"I'm telling the truth. No fantasies, no erotic dreams—well, almost no erotic dreams. No conscious daydreams. You have to remember how successfully we were walled off. After a while, most signs of spontaneity disappear. We were taught not to embrace anyone, not to have sensual feelings. We didn't hug, kiss, hold hands, dance, or even sit close. It was still possible for seminarians to leave the 'world' and be indoctrinated with a whole set of in-hibitions. I don't know. I had a head start, so the Church just reinforced my own inclinations."

"And it worked?"

"Yes and no. It worked within the bounds I set up. After ordination, I taught at a seminary, indoctrinating others into my obsessions. Then I was sent to Rome, into even greater seclusion, into even greater inhibition. But the rare times I was physically close to a woman, all manner of difficult sensations arose."

"So to speak."

"So to speak."

"What of your fellow priests. I understand they're not so successful at managing their impulses?"

I lay on my back with my arms folded behind my head. Jean supported herself on one elbow. Sleep was banished. She wanted the story. "Well, you know, the sixties happened. Young priests were bombarded with sensuality, open sexuality, expected to be able to counsel others, put in situations of closeness during retreats, in their ministries, which they weren't prepared for. The Church remains a pre-Freudian society in which abstinence is seen as a higher state, closer to God. Sent out into a world where sex is assumed to be necessary to a healthy life, most found the spiritual benefits of celibacy no match for constant temptation. The heterosexual priests left, ran away with the organist, or the divorcee they were counseling, or a woman they met on a retreat."

"I remember a few of those stories."

"Well, there were a lot of them. Behind them fell the seminarians. What did the Church have to offer? A life that was seen not as one of sacrifice and honor but a life that was peculiar, out of step with reality. That left a lot of young men and a lot of priests who were comfortable in an all-male society, who were choosing it because it was an all-male society. The Church couldn't afford to lose them. With whom would they replace them? And Rome is intransigent about allowing priests to marry, so it's a standoff. When there is scandal, the hierarchy simply moves the priest to another parish. No counseling, no careful eye on his behavior. It's a suicidal policy."

"But don't they still see abstinence as holy? As the only cure for everything from AIDS to teen pregnancies?"

"What do you expect them to do? Change an institution which was founded on its own immutability? Most Catholics haven't gotten over the change from the Latin Mass. Think they'll suddenly accept homosexuality and abortion?"

"Why not?"

"They might risk losing what set them apart from other religions. And they might find that if Rome bent, it might break. If it changed an important doctrine, then maybe you didn't have to obey its teaching on other important doctrines. Maybe anybody's conscience was as good as anybody else's."

"What would be so wrong about that?"

"That would leave them stranded."

"Stranded?"

"With a doctrine of compassion, understanding, forgiveness, real forgiveness of sin, in a world they want to command with the male values of self-discipline and guilt."

"What about you, Gabriel?"

"I am the worst kind. I didn't feel I had a lot of sexuality to give up. Until now, I never considered it, well, almost never. I was ambitious and the Church offered unlimited advancement."

"So does Wall Street and the U.S. Marines."

"I guess their uniforms didn't appeal to me. I always felt separate from others. I don't know how to do otherwise. The Church validated my intention to be alone and left me alone. I didn't feel lonely or alienated, there was a whole tradition which said that it wasn't strange to want that. In fact it made me superior, it made me valuable."

"Didn't your fellow priests come on to you?"

"No."

"Never?"

"Everyone has been more than content to keep their distance. The students and faculty where I taught probably considered me a prig or worse. My fellows in Rome were mostly like me, ambitious, asexual, and hostile. Most of the priests who are in trouble are in the front lines in parishes, trying, or not trying, to keep their hands off the altar boys."

"What happened, where did it all go wrong?"

I laughed. "Saint Paul, Augustine, Jerome. 'It's better to marry than to burn.' Bad enough, but it got worse. Paul, the creep, and Augustine, the profligate penitent, hated women and hated the body. Add Aquinas to the mixture, stir in some Neoplatonic crap in the Renaissance and you have a religion washed of all real mysticism, a mind-body split that becomes an unbridgeable gulf, an innate mistrust of women which spills over to the Church's view of Mary, and a bunch of pederasts in cassocks because the normal and healthy left to pursue normal and healthy hetero- or homosexual relations somewhere else. It started very early, this hatred of the body and hatred of the feminine, but it never worked. The history of the Church is the history of public pronouncement and private scandal. My God, there were the 'papal nephews,' which were what the bastard sons of the popes were called. Women couldn't go to confession without being molested by the priests, which is why we have confessionals with screened partitions now. Priests up until recently were 'married,' often openly, and the Church quietly condoned these relationships because it kept down the incidents of rape and scandal."

"Jesus."

"There are two things that can happen. A reformer can appear, gather a mass audience to himself, and change the Church from the inside. The liberationists have tried and been silenced. At least they have fared better than they might have a few centuries ago. Of course my job was to keep a mystical event from triggering such a movement. The other thing that could happen happened during the Middle Ages. The Church was split apart by schism, two popes, even three popes, all of them drunks, libertines, and murderers claiming to be the legitimate Vicar of Christ. It caused chaos. A chaos that threatened the whole concept of the Church. When the bishops left Avignon after the schism, one boasted that he left a brothel that extended from one end of the city to the other."

"There is a third possibility."

"What?"

"The Church will cease to be relevant and simply disappear."

"Never happen."

"How can you be so sure?"

"The Church has been irrelevant for about five hundred years and it is still a dominant force in the world. A nice anachronism, good for tourism, bad for people. But now I don't know. There is no godless communism to fight, to push against. In this country, even the devout think for themselves, a bad sign. But look at the East where the Church bought Poland and is making great gains in parts of Russia. It makes the Fatimists real nervous."

"Gabriel, you're weird."

"You know, everyone knows, the conversion of Russia is one condition for the Apocalypse. According to Mary, at least the Mary of three Portuguese peasants in 1917."

"Gabriel, what are we going to do?"

"Stay under the covers and discuss theology."

"Oh well, OK."

"That's not theology."

"Thank God."

CHAPTER
THIRTY-SIX

Our fear became commonplace and then it disappeared. Our love grew stronger until it was stronger than everything except the future. The future was the uninvited guest at every meal, the silent critic in every conversation. We wanted to know everything about each other, as though that knowledge could stand in the way of doubt, as though it could be a barricade against time and destiny. We made food, and made love, and talked. I record our conversations because they are the only testament that I was once a man. I relive our love in my imagination, but the fragments, while sweet, only prove that past intimacy becomes identical with unbearable pain.

Jean's desire to understand the contradictions inherent in my life became insatiable. "So come on, Gabriel, is it all that bad, is the Church hopeless?"

"Yes and no."

"Typical, Gabriel, typical. But I'm not a reporter trying to drag a statement out of you."

"Sorry, it's a conditioned reflex, I'm Pavlov's prelate. The Church has had two thousand years in which to tie its own hands with official pronouncements that are supposed to arrive with the direct intervention of the Holy Spirit."

"All that infallible stuff?"

"Yes, all that infallibility. It had been implied for centuries, one pope after another affirming or confirming that he was the representative on earth not of St. Peter but of Christ himself. Finally, Pius IX decreed it a few months before Italy was reunified and his papal states were taken away. Sort of a going away present to himself. For years, even though he was still known as *il Papa Re*, he had been losing temporal power. A pope hadn't excommunicated an emperor in years. The loss of the papal states was a last blow. So Pius IX made sure his spiritual power was left intact. Infallibility does the trick nicely, don't you think? It had only been a few years since he had declared the Immaculate Conception."

"So he's the one."

"He's the one. Of course, the infallibility was retroactive, making all popes since Peter infallible, which makes most change impossible. The pope can't undo a mistake of a predecessor or seem to make any change at all. He can only hold the line."

"OK, I get the depressing part, Gabriel. What about the yes part. What about the part that isn't hopeless."

"Well, I was once part of a group that worked overtime trying to keep the Church in South Africa from either martyring itself in the cause of liberty or coming out for apartheid."

"Don't tell me you've done some good things?"

"Neutral at least. Anyway, all the African hierarchy was invited to Rome. Good public relations while we worked behind the scenes."

"Is this the good part?"

"I'm getting to it. Well, a rather progressive parish just down the hill from where I lived in Rome, Santa Maria in Trastevere, decided to have a Mass for peace in Africa. Everyone was invited and the African delegation was given a free hand in presenting the liturgy.

"The church was packed. Now it's not a huge basilica but, to me, it's the most beautiful church in the world and the closest to reflecting the spirit of Mary, Byzantine mosaics with scenes from her life, a wonderful golden mosaic of Mary seated next to Christ.

"So the church was filled with Italians and Africans, young and old, filled with true Christian zeal and love.

Six African women led the procession to the beat of drums and gourds, an unbelievable procession of twenty or thirty bishops, a couple of cardinals following the women up the main aisle. And the women were wearing wrapped skirts of African fabric and, well, shaking their hips to the syncopated rhythms."

"Sounds kind of sexy."

"It was holy. The church filled with unexpected and beautiful music. The procession alone took twenty minutes. Then the liturgy: an African bishop blessing the parishioners with a long brush dipped in holy water instead of an aspergillum, with a gesture of blessing and a real experience of the water; the women processing again around a priest carrying the Bible over his head, as if to say, Here comes the good news, here comes the Word, while everyone sang the Kyrie as though it were an African love song. By this time, the faithful were swaying in time with the music and the Mass went on like this; another procession, this time of hosts along with baskets of fruit and flowers as if to say, This is food and drink indeed, not an abstraction but spiritual nourishment."

"I've never heard you talk this way. I love it."

"I don't always remember to have hope. Anyway, after communion, olive branches were handed around to everyone and everyone sang a prayer for peace in Italian and waved the olive branches above their heads. I even caught a few Italian bishops tapping their feet to the beat of the drums. Finally, a bishop from each African nation lit a candle for peace and then, and this is the part I helped set the ground rules for, the white South African bishop embraced the black bishop. Everybody waved their olive branches and cheered. The African women led us out. My God, cheers in a church. For hours after, the young people of the parish danced and sang outside the rectory."

"I understand, Gabriel."

"Look, I didn't really understand then. I was relieved all was going according to plan. I am just learning to understand that experience, to see the love and hope implied in it. A lot has had to happen to me to make me see. And even now, my feelings are tempered with the knowledge of how much better off Africa would be if it had never heard of Rome. Yet it was the most beautiful and spiritual Mass I have ever witnessed."

"And it happened under the watchful eye of Mary."

"And it happened under the watchful eye of Mary."

CHAPTER
THIRTY-SEVEN

There were only a few cans of food left, half a bottle of whiskey, and some wine her friend was keeping for a special occasion. We couldn't just walk into a store and buy food. We had created a vacuum that more and more of the media would like to fill, a vacuum that the Vatican would also rush into. I sat for hours looking out the window at the place where the dirt road emerged from the trees. The house was California ranch style with mullioned windows and stained cedar siding that gave it almost a New England grandeur. The furnishings were sparse and monochromatic, but unlike most modern houses there were bookcases filled with books. There was a modern kitchen of stainless steel and oak, but it looked as though it was built to create pleasurable events beyond the ability of its inhabitant to enjoy properly.

Jean busied herself with trying to find food, with what became obsessive cleaning and, when that was finished, pacing. She found the remnants of an overgrown garden that yielded a few zucchini, an onion, and a handful of basil. She found wild strawberries and blackberries, each discovery accompanied by triumphant shouts that became both more infrequent and more forced.

She started to weed the garden, then dug into the flower beds, pruning the roses and fruit trees with a ferocious passion. She wore tights and a man's shirt, tying the shirttails into a knot at her waist. I sat out on the small terrace and watched her while I worked on the notes that have become this history. Once in a while our eyes would meet and she would smile or make a face and continue working. My heart ached as I watched, ached with longing at her beauty, ached with fear because I knew it could not last much longer.

Miraculously, Jean found enough food to keep us fed. But the fare went from salads and vegetables to minestrone which became more and more like broth. She sang while she worked, a few tortured arias from *Madame Butterfly*, yet I could see the worry begin to pull at the corners of her mouth, I could see in her love of gardening, of the land, a struggle to regain her nature. She began to dig more and more furiously without looking up, and when she did, she did not look in my direction except to shake her head and continue working.

I began to walk the perimeter of the house, peering into the undergrowth looking for signs that we had been discovered. I memorized each place like a scholar, noted the singing of birds, the barking of dogs in the distance.

I found myself consumed with anger. Anger at my superiors, at the way my flaws had been used by them. Anger at myself for accepting so long the constraints of a false nature. And anger that hope was to be measured in moments, moments that moved us inexorably apart.

CHAPTER
THIRTY-EIGHT

"Gabriel, in case you didn't notice, the soup was a little thin tonight, and that half a glass of wine was it, *basta.*"

"I know, I know." All the flowers in the garden had opened, and there were wildflowers on the hillside below the house. We sat on the stairs of the porch and watched the light die over Tomales Bay.

"I don't think you do know. I love you, which I frankly never thought I could say to a man again. But I feel the future closing in. The future should be ahead of us, and now the future is crowding in all around. Gabriel, this is so hard. I've never done this before and I think I'm making a mess of it. Please forgive me. I mean, I used to just leave in the middle of the night, or take a lover and make it more and more obvious until he got the point, or do something outrageous just to get things rolling. But I want you to understand. It's so important you understand."

I knew what Jean also knew. That for her I would keep silent, for her I would disappear, change lives, definitions. That clear spring night we watched the silence and the darkness. I wished again for the coldness and ruthlessness I had fed on. They would not come. I tried to imagine my life without love, without change. I could not. I felt only the beginnings of a kinship with and deep sadness for all humans.

When it was fully dark, she touched my arm, kissed me lightly on the cheek, and went into the house. Later

I went in also. I tried to read. I wrote and paced when the thoughts wouldn't come. Finally, in the last hour of the night, I slid into bed beside Jean and fell into a dreamless sleep. I awoke the next morning pierced by the light of sunrise and she was gone.

CHAPTER
THIRTY-NINE

I packed my few things carefully. Since the first inkling of trouble, I had begun to hoard cash. I counted it. It was just enough for what I would attempt. Then I called the reporter, Jonas Quigley, and pitched my deal. He laughed a hard whiskey laugh. "You always have a few surprises left, don't you?"

"Do we have a deal?"

"Why should I help you? I could wait with the jackals and still get a damn good story. Might even find some trace of who you really are."

"You know it's a better story this way. You also know there is no trace left, a very cold trail indeed."

"Still doesn't leave you with much to bargain with, does it?"

"Perhaps just enough."

"I gotta say, you may be no saint, but you have faith."

"Is it enough faith?"

"I'll get back to you."

"I'm afraid there is little time."

"Gimme an hour."

Jonas Quigley called back an hour later. We had a deal. A story for him about the Vatican think tank, what I had been doing the last few years, the Mary story, everything. In exchange, he and his organization would get me out of the country and back to Italy with some kind of cover.

"What are you afraid of exactly? I mean it's a church, isn't it?"

"Indulge me."

"What makes you more than a paranoid with a scary story? With what I know already I could maybe get you a spot on Oprah, maybe Geraldo, sandwiched between some fifteen-year-old cheerleader who murdered her boyfriend on a whim and a whiff, some mechanic from Decatur who claims some alien being had been measuring his dick, and a housewife from East Peoria who remembers under hypnosis that the devil made her rip the arms off babies. I mean I want a story, declarative sentences, chapter and verse, a place I can dig and not come up covered with shit. Do you follow me?"

"Who are Oprah and Geraldo?"

"I forgot. Out of a hundred and fifty million people, you are maybe the only one who wouldn't have heard of them. What I'm trying to say is that I work for a magazine, a rare thing these days, a magazine that prints pieces by real investigative reporters, not unsubstantiated rumors spread by a bunch of sociopaths who want to splatter their sickness over the airwaves. I've watched you real close and there seems to be someone at home under the collar. So I'm going to have to trust you on the paranoia angle. But it worries me.

"Just so you know," he continued, "I'm the house expert on the Church. I cut my teeth on the mysterious death of John Paul, the assassination attempt on John Paul II, the Banco Ambrosiano scam, Sindona, Franklin National, the murder of Calvi, the twisted life of Archbishop Marcinkus. I've been to Brazil, Nicaragua, El Salvador covering liberation theology and the assassination of Romero by that creep D'Aubisson. So I've been around. I'm no choirboy. Shoot straight with me and we have a deal. Tart it up, or play me for a fool, and I'll sit around and watch, just to see if your fears are real."

"I'm not willing to test my theses at this moment."

"Test my theses, I like that, I like that. You know, you sling the shit with the best."

"I assure you, Mr. Quigley, I have a story for you, a story you will not get anywhere else. In exchange, I need your help. I am not particularly paranoid. What I have done myself, and have seen done by others, leads me to believe I have something to fear."

"OK, OK. Jesus, this is one for the books. You think they murdered John Paul I?"

"I have no conclusive proof. Any proof was buried with him. Remember, there was no autopsy. He was about to clean up a few Vatican scandals, beginning the next day. The coincidence is food for thought. My story includes much more subtle interventions. The investigators I worked with are not thugs. We usually found ways to make the power of our office felt without resorting to extrarational means."

"I'll pick you up in an hour. This ought to be goddamn interesting. I like it. Where the hell are you? Everyone's been chasing his tail out here."

"Then we have a deal?"

"Yeah, yeah, we have a deal. I pick you up, we'll talk on the way to the airport, OK?"

I told him where to pick me up and hung up. I looked around in panic. The banal tidiness of the house, the quiet beauty of the day only intensified my fear. I was to join the damned who had lost everything. I had fallen from the wheel.

CHAPTER
FORTY

Jonas Quigley almost crashed a few times on the way
to the airport. He would turn his bloodshot eyes toward
me in disbelief, turning back to the road just in time.
He was about forty-five, a huge man with a permanent
wince, as though everything I could tell him would
only cause him trouble and pain.

"I mean," he said, "I was a fucking altar boy, for chris-
sakes. Lost the faith about the same time I lost my vir-
ginity, but until I started following the Church for a
living I still had some respect, felt a little guilty for leaving, you know? But this stuff makes me nuts."

"Just try to get me to the airport in one piece. Start
with what I have told you, start with Signorelli, trace a
few of the leads. You'll have your story. It shouldn't surprise you—the Church is a large organization and be-
haves like one."

"You're something of a coldblooded bastard, aren't
you?"

"I was."

"And the Mary stuff is on the level? I mean, you seem
like a tough guy, a lot of starch in the collar. You come
here to burn a few witches, which is nothing for you,
and you get turned into some kind of mystic. I follow
you up to a certain line, then you cross it."

"I've told you my story. I was nobody's fool but my
own as an investigator. The fact that I have told you my
story, that I feel the need to tell my story, necessitates
a complete break with my past."

He whistled a long low whistle and kept his eyes on

the road. We rode in silence for a while, then he reached into his coat pocket and handed me an envelope. In it was a one-way ticket to Milan and a passport. "Cost us an arm and a leg, but what the hell." He grinned a lopsided grin. "It's a hell of a story."

I looked out the window at the gleaming new buildings behind whose implacable façades the dim and macabre outlines of an uncertain future were forming.

"We're almost there. What about Andreotti and the death of Moro? What about Licio Gelli and P2, the Bologna train station? What about Opus Dei?" His eyes shone with an almost sinister light as he again turned to me, almost missing the single-lane exit to the airport.

"Our office was not directly political, we worked secretly and alone. Those stories have already received a lot of attention. Opus Dei is a name that surfaces at odd moments. It is masterful at infiltrating the highest government and civilian offices. Much of what it does is secret. I was privy to no information that is not already common knowledge. Except," I said as an afterthought, "you might spend some time looking into the background of a man in London named Henry Throckmorton."

"Damn," he said as he threaded his way to Departures. He stopped the car and gave me one final searching look, "You going to be OK? I mean you're on your own. You're dressed like a priest. God knows you still act like one. But you're invisible, the name on the passport won't do squat for you in Italy. You don't have much in the way of skills outside of being a scholarly shit."

"I'll send you a card when I have it figured out. For a short time, a wandering priest won't attract attention."

"Yeah, well, as ol' Satchel said, 'Don't look back, they might be gaining."

"Who is Satchel?"

"Forget it."

CHAPTER
FORTY-ONE

By the time I arrived at the Torontola train station the next evening, I had been traveling for twenty-four hours. I had waited interminably in train stations, a solitary figure in a priest's dark suit.

I walked outside in the gathering dusk. My heart leapt and I let out my breath for the first time in days. I was back in Italy. I saw the streets open before me; the *forno*, the *alimentari, feramenta, farmacia*. An old man rolled up an awning, another swept the sidewalk in front of his shop. The evening was consumed in comfortable rituals. Above the small town of Torontola loomed the brooding presence of Cortona, its stone streets pitched at steep angles toward the church of Santa Margarita, another who had made the transition from sensuality to self-mortification. She had cut her face to mar its beauty and ensure her asceticism. She cast her son into a monastery and then entered another herself. I had to smile. I was no saint by any standards and my transition was from asceticism to sensuality.

I took a cab into the center of Cortona, a cab ride back to the past. Suddenly I was not tired, not hunted, not weighted down by the millstones of guilt and remorse. I walked the stone streets, caught up in their brooding. Cortona, Assisi, Orvieto, Roma. I would make my stand on territory I understood as though I had lived there for centuries. I had had enough of cities with streets laid out at right angles.

The Etruscans built the first walls of Cortona, a large section of which still stands. From this hill, one could manage an exile. From the edge of the city opened an endless vista of olive orchards, vineyards, and the patchwork of tilled earth that had been fecund for thirty centuries. Although in Tuscany, Cortona is the portal of Umbria, and it was with a certain irony that I faced a new life in a former papal state. I could feel the presence of St. Francis, could see the gentility he extended to everyone, his love of simplicity, and his progressive fervor that spiced the politics of the region. I sat for a long time in a cafe just off the piazza and caught up with the political scandals, with the terrorist and Mafia bombings, with the struggles of a nation that was really still an uneasy alliance of city-states trying to hold a center that had been inexorably shifting to the north. Where once this penchant for chaos had annoyed me, now it felt like balm. When they finish with the political system, I mused, perhaps they will begin on the Church.

I went to the telephone booth in the back of the bar and phoned Poncarelli. He was surprised not only to hear from me, but to hear of my exile. I told him I would come by bus to Umbria the next day, but he insisted that I stay with him that night.

His ancient Fiat Cinquecento sputtered to a stop in front of the cafe an hour later. He disentangled himself from it and hugged me. "Gabriel, you look like hell. I have often thought of your dilemma, but I thought you would make a slow descent into living like the rest of us. You seem to have plunged."

"I was pushed."

"Indeed. But it was inevitable. I knew someday you would discover a heart beating unheeded in your chest. The results are always unpredictable. Unfortunately, the response of our superiors is always the same. Ah, but you had a higher perch to fall from, and I'm afraid you made a much publicized fall."

"It is about to get worse. I gave a tell-all interview just before I left. An interview that will cause widespread apoplexy. I'm afraid there is not a single bridge I could recross."

"Just as well, just as well. As I wrote you, you did me a favor by deepening my exile. I was deluding myself that I could resurrect an ecstatic tradition, deluding myself that I had a place in the Church at all. I love the priesthood, and I loved my parishioners deeply, but how can one be a part of such nonsense? Not even you, the cream of the Vatican crop, could stomach it."

We drove through the now darkened fields toward the Niccone valley. Poncarelli had become, if anything, more burly and self-assured. He wore jeans and a striped shirt. He now worked as a stonemason for an Umbrian contractor who rebuilt abandoned farmhouses for foreign owners.

"The history of it all is a little odd, Gabriel. The *contadini* supported Mussolini as the agent of their redemption. He did nothing for them. But he was a symbol of the futurism that ended their servitude, a feudal system that had managed to survive unchanged for centuries. Rather than run electricity and sewer lines to the peasants' houses, the Fascists moved them off the land into concrete-block apartment houses. It was their leap into the future. The old life was nothing, the old ways were nothing. They were promised gleaming prizes—the factory and empire. Who would have chosen differently? Sure, they knew every inch of the land, and sure, it was the most beautiful and fertile in the world, and sure, they were able to scratch a living out of it and be nearly self-sufficient."

"It would seem easy to be self-sufficient here."

"They made everything themselves, their own olive oil, wine, prosciutto, bread, grew their own vegetables. And, of course, they didn't own the land and owed at least half their crops to the *padrone*, who lived in a castle while they lived in these farmhouses where the animals lived downstairs and provided the only heat. But if there was a freeze or the animals got sick, or a child got sick, they might be wiped out. So who wouldn't abandon land that was both a blessing and a scourge and move to these new communities of concrete and steel and work for wages making machines for the state?

"You know, it only takes a few years of neglect before a house and its land are doomed to be ruins. Years of animal shit downstairs becomes great soil for blackberries, blackthorn, all manner of vines which push at the roof tiles. Soon the rains and snow rot a few support beams, and sections of roof and floor collapse. Ivy and dampness loosen the mortar between the stones, which is mostly sand anyway. The peasants who built these houses were master masons but they had little money for cement, and so the walls are breached and suddenly you have a ruin.

"The land suffers an almost biblical enchantment. The blackberry vines and the thorn bushes pull the new olive shoots down into perpetual twilight where they can exist but never flower, never bear fruit. Everything becomes overgrown because it had once been tilled. You understand? Walk out into the *bosco* and it is a carpet of rotting leaves and wildflowers and, here in Umbria, chestnut and scrub oak. You only find the land cursed when men clear the land, use it up, and then leave.

"The land is beautiful but it is associated with an evil system, a system of servitude and perpetual poverty with no hope of advancement, no hope that a child could aspire to anything more than his father did. And fascism, whatever else it was, was a radical social engineer, moved masses of people off the land, changed the system forever, leaving much of the land enchanted.

"Modernity meant embracing war and war also is a great social engineer. Among other things, you need factories to make the stuff of war and that accelerates the exodus. Whoever isn't fighting for the new glorious state is working in the factories making vast fortunes for men who are not called *padrone*. Except now you live in a concrete box with electric lights and running water but no land when all you have known for centuries is the land.

"Of course the war is a disaster, fascism another disaster, and after the war whoever isn't dead rebuilds, but the enchantment of the land persists. We were taken up by a futurism that was not tied to ideology, not tied to the state. And because of the strength of the Communist party, social structures are put in place, educational systems for everyone, health care, pensions. And because of the weakness of communism, it is all in the service of industrialization for its own sake, consumption for its own sake. And because of the strength of capitalism, the country is rapidly industrialized and there is money for everyone and everyone consumes and lives in taller and taller towers. And because of the weakness of capitalism, there are no controls and no planning and the air and the beaches and the rivers and the forest are nearly destroyed until we are sick of it all.

"A few foreigners who have made enough money and lived enough life to become sick to death of it come to Italy, buy the ruins, and rebuild them. For many years the Italians think they are crazy. Why would anyone want what are still the symbols of their shameful past, their *vergogna*? The foreigners buy them cheap. For them, it is one last chance to escape the future they have been trapped into building. And slowly they lift the enchantment, open up the land, plant fruit trees and olive trees. The government finally realizes they are about to ruin everything that is Italy in order to modernize it. So they make zones where no new buildings can be built and remake the forests and slowly the land returns to its splendor. Except the enchantment has one more level. The old stone houses are chopped into apartments and rented to other foreigners and the land becomes grounds and garden to be looked at and kept static, but not worked, not made fruitful. I am here, as irony would have it, to work to make this come about. To lift the enchantment although I know it is qualified by sadness at what was lost forever."

"Which was just a system that oppressed people."

"Yes, that system is gone, an oppressive system, but replaced with like evils—greed and materialism."

"But now with unions, pensions, health care. Not unimportant changes."

"But they could have instituted changes and left the life intact."

"Of course. But you're asking to rewrite the history of the last forty years."

"Here's our turn."

The house was nestled in a wooded area about two miles up a tortuous gravel road. It had been built in the seventeenth century in the peasant style. The stones had either been found when the land was originally cleared or quarried with primitive tools from the indigenous sandstone. There was now a large kitchen, a living room with a huge fireplace and two bedrooms.

"A friend lets me stay here for practically nothing. He started out renting to tourists like everyone else and then couldn't stomach it. He's rich enough to do what he wants and in exchange I am rebuilding his barn in my spare time.

"You must be exhausted."

He went into the kitchen and poured two large glasses of wine. "You must eat something. We must celebrate our freedom, our meeting again under different circumstances." He laughed and tossed back the wine.

Then he made a *pasta all'amatriciana*, opened another bottle of Umbrian wine, sat at the table and said, "Now you must tell me your story."

We drank and talked for a long time. At some point in my story he laughed and shook his head, then stood up and went to a cupboard, returning with a dusty bottle of grappa. The first taste was like a sip of bottled fire. The second brought a warm flush. Many times he stopped me, made me repeat something that had been said or done, grunted, drank, then motioned me to continue.

"You have been writing this down, have you not?"

"I started a few months ago."

"You must. Keep the writing always with you in an envelope addressed to me. If you are in trouble slip it into a box and I will know." Poncarelli looked at me intently. "Your story must not be lost. Those jackals must never get the last word." We raised our glasses and drank.

CHAPTER
FORTY-TWO

The days were bright and hot. The scirocco blew, flowers bloomed, bright perfect fruit hung from the trees. All day we worked on the walls of a farmhouse a few miles away. I mixed mortar, carried stones, chiseled them to make them fit, and moved scaffolding as work progressed. My hands, the soft flesh of the scholar, were cut and scraped and then calloused by the work. My back ached, I was thirsty all the time.

Poncarelli and I worked with a crew of masons. There was Camillo, who had a classic Etruscan face and the patience of a Zen monk. There was Rigo, more typically Umbrian, nervous and brusque until he knew you, then more generous with knowledge but no less brusque and formal. He had an encyclopedic knowledge of the local plants and trees. There was Alfredo, who kept to himself, rarely speaking except to answer direct questions and then with two or three words. They were all over sixty and had worked together for twenty or thirty years. We worked hard, from 7:30 to 5:30 with a morning break and an hour for lunch. I spent my lunches listening to Rigo talk of his olive trees, his vineyards, of mushroom hunting under the oak trees in the forest, or giving instructions on how to cook the birds he shot on the weekends. Camillo punctuated Rigo's monologues with a simple *capito*. I was sure Camillo had heard it all a thousand times and hardly listened, showing just enough interest to be polite. Poncarelli and I usually ate in silence, and sometimes dozed off for a few minutes before work resumed.

As I became used to the work, I slowly relaxed and shed some of my Roman nervousness and impatience. Work became a kind of retreat, a meditation. When a wall was finished, it almost seemed to be the result of a process of thought, of will, as much as a physical accomplishment. My fellow workers accepted me without question, without qualification. Our work became one harmonious act. Although work was always done to the accompaniment of jokes and mock insults, there was never the discord of competition, of ambition; never the pall of melancholy and discontent that hung over the scholar. These men had never left Umbria, had rarely left that valley.

On Sundays I would often borrow Poncarelli's Fiat and tour Umbria: Assisi, Città di Castello, Perugia, Orvieto, San Sepulcro, Angiari. I would wander the streets alone, punctuating my peregrinations with an espresso or a vermouth. Sometimes Poncarelli would accompany me and we would sit for hours and argue about esoterica.

"Gabriel, I worry about you. You still work like a man obsessed, like it is self-mortification. It is very un-Italian, even unhealthy. Work must be a pleasure, you must become the wall, lose yourself in the solidity of the stone, in creating pleasing shapes. You still want to guide the stone with your will alone, to break yourself against the wall. This imparts too much tension. Your walls look guilty, lonely, melancholic. What should I expect of a man whose heroes and heroines were all burned at the stake? You must put it all behind you."

"Have you managed to put your Beguines, your ecstatics behind you, Dominic?"

"But that is quite different. My poor ecstatics did not have to be grilled in order to see God. It was part of their common experience. I am not that anxious to take up permanent residence, just visit for a time. Especially if the last thing I smell is burning flesh, mine."

"I seem to have developed an interest in the burned," I laughed. "But it is an accident, I assure you. In my present circumstances, it is ironic that they were all burned by the Church or with its sanction. Does that make them martyrs or not?"

"You must admit that the Church was only the failed mask of political expediency. Joan, now Joan was a case. Imagine, she was only nineteen when she died. And at nineteen, with the direction of a few angelic voices, she was just about the best general France was to see until Napoleon."

"Who was a Corsican."

"Exactly. Peasant girl of sixteen winning battles in the name of God. She did not wait upon the pleasure of her voices. She seemed able to converse with them at will. You must admit, her angelic and saintly presences had a wonderful grasp of military strategy."

"They seemed to desert her in the end."

"True, but falling into English hands has never been pleasant for the French. After all, what choice did the English have but to burn her? They were backing the other side of the schism. If her voices were really messages from God, then England was on the side of the Antichrist. Joan had to be a witch, and there were even respected clerics who devised tests, medical and verbal, to determine if the voices were not demons posing as angels."

"Yes, they sent teams of physicians to determine if she were a *virgo intacta*, reasoning that a virgin was a more proper vessel of divine inspiration. Oddly enough, no one ever seemed to doubt that she heard voices, they only fought about their origin. I mean, the facts to more modern minds seem almost surreal."

"But Gabriel, the history of the schism is also surreal. Dual baptisms, confirmations, marriages, boat blessings, indulgences, a whole dual religious organization. Think of the cost! Who was to know which side was right? The proponents of each were bloodthirsty, decadent, greedy, and brutal. What test could they devise for these men that might show God's favor? Think of that! Poor Joan!"

With such conversation, we spent our exile, our calloused hands gesturing wildly. I was always conscious that it was an exile. I did not yet feel hunted. I felt almost invisible, as though I were alive but no longer involved, a supernumerary. I wrote my history but already it seemed distant, as though the story had been told to me by an acquaintance I barely trusted. Only the desire to understand my experience drove me on.

It was then I began making the pilgrimage to Siena whenever possible. It was then I first seized on the mosaic of the wheel of fortune. During the day, my hands were occupied with earth and stone, with architecture and engineering, but my mind began to turn it all over and over again. I had to force myself to notice the beauty around me. Poncarelli would jokingly hold a ripe fig in front of my face or push me out of the house and into the forest to hunt mushrooms.

A man who has lived by ambition, has sacrificed his instincts for it, does not leave it behind easily. I felt my life had been wasted, that I had failed at the profession I had chosen.

Dominic, however, still had friends in Rome. Not men of influence but priests who worked in the shadow of St. Peter's. Once a month he went to Rome to visit his friends and catch up with Vatican gossip. He always returned to Umbria shaking his head at the folly he found there.

"To tell the truth, Gabriel, I am happy to be quit with it. I am a peasant in my heart, and this valley is as close to God as any place on earth. My walls are my prayers. The Roman church is all empty politics and compromise. I heard from a curial secretary, who was proud of himself, that they had succeeded in having a paper on population expunged from the Rio conference. Proud! Is there wine in the house? Let's drink. What is there to eat? It is only out of perversity I show my face in Rome. A priest forever . . ."

I built a fire of pruned olive and cherry branches. Poncarelli, brandishing a knife like a street fighter, boned a small leg of young lamb, a *coccia di abbacchio;* put chopped garlic, red pepper flakes, and rosemary on the inside and tied it in a roll. While it grilled over the coals, I made a sauce of garlic, oil, and fresh porcini. Dominic picked lettuce and beans from the garden.

"On my last trip to Rome," he said, "I talked with an old friend who works for an Italian magazine. They picked up on a story in a small American journal. It detailed the inner workings of the very secret organization that once employed you. Enlightening reading. Weeping Madonnas in the Abruzzi, crop circles in the Midlands, apparitions in California. A Monsignor Signorelli was mentioned, deep scandals hinted at, a nexus of conspiracy involving certain lay orders and Sir Henry Throckmorton, the champion of the British pound.

"Of course, the editor just laughed and buried the piece. Your name was not mentioned. My friend, however, says there is the wailing and gnashing of teeth in certain circles. An enormous monsignor is suddenly unavailable for comment, and the shadowy Englishman has decided to take a long cruise. His creditors are not amused, included among them a bank that seems to have its own intelligence service. How secure, exactly, was your departure from the States?"

The circumstances of the interview with Jonas Quigley and my flight to Milan came back to me. I laughed. "I would have loved to see Signorelli waddling out of the Vatican."

"How secure was your departure? My God, Gabriel, your enemies have the Italian intelligence services in their back pocket."

"It was as secret as possible. I traveled on a valid passport, but not under my own name. I took a train here."

"Perhaps you should have left a few holes in your story."

"Quigley was no fool, he had half the story already. Besides I did leave a few things out. Rumors I had heard. Things I hadn't any proof of."

"Like?"

"Like a few new possibilities of who hired Ali Agça, a rumor that Throckmorton was seen talking to Roberto Calvi the night he died, rumors concerning Cardinals Spellman and Cody, a few scraps about Monsignor Hüdel and the rat lines."

"Pass the wine, I'm suddenly very thirsty. How long do you think it is safe here? This isn't Siberia. It's only two hours from Rome."

"My usefulness to them is over. I talked and then disappeared. Why should they expend the energy to find me? They still have the power to keep the story from spreading. In a week or two, it will be dead. I can't hurt them anymore."

"Magistrates all over Italy are discovering their *palle*, politicians are going to jail, and they're singing arias once they're in custody. So far, the Church isn't implicated in this fresh round of housecleaning, but you could change that."

"I told you, I said everything I had to say."

"I know you think you're in limbo, stuck somewhere between heaven and hell, but you must realize, they don't know how much you know, they don't know that you can't substantiate those rumors you speak of. They will hunt for you, not with every resource at their disposal, but relentlessly."

"The longer I am here, the more invisible I feel. If what you say is true and Signorelli has gone, perhaps no one is left who remembers."

"Throckmorton remembers. It is true, they will sleep badly for a long time. On the other hand, the time is ripe for pigs like the P2. All Italy remembers the Bologna train station, the attempts to destabilize the government. Just the other day there was the bombing of the Uffizi. Politicians do not love a vacuum. Everyone in Rome thinks the P2 scandal left many members in high places waiting for their chance. Now might be that chance. They do not need to hear rumors that rake the still-live coals of old stories. You must be clear about the fact that you are part of something that threatens many dangerous men with exposure."

"What am I supposed to do? Here I appear on no government rolls, we are paid cash by the American woman. I no longer have the sloping shoulders and pale flesh of the priest. I have coffee on occasion in Umbertide. I frequent the market. No one takes notice of me. I have even begun to slip into dialect on occasion."

"But we are still *stranieri*. This valley is remote, but it is also static. Except for the Moroccans who come for the tobacco harvest and a few tourists, neither of which you clearly are, anyone who hasn't been here for a few generations is still an outsider. They treat us well but we stand out, if a professional should wish to investigate. After all, the *carabinieri* routinely set up a roadblock at Mercatale, which is just a few kilometers down the road. It would take only a polite suggestion for them to watch for you on the road. This is a benign country, but it supports more police for less reason than just about any nation on earth. You have seen them on the road to Città di Castello, on the road to Cortona off the A1. True they look bored, true they would rather stop an attractive woman just to see if she has pretty legs, true they earn their reputation for lack of intelligence, but they are ubiquitous and they do have radios."

"I have nowhere to go."

"I have begun to think of the problem. A solution is not far away. Think of yourself as Jonah."

"Jonah?"

"Even though he was never burned at the stake, you must have heard of him."

"Of course. But what has Jonah to do with me?"

"You must hide in the belly of the beast."

"Rome?"

"Rome."

"How?"

"Rome is a confusion of clerics arriving and departing from all parts of the world. No one can keep track of them. Of the thousands of priests only a few are attached formally to the Vatican. There are institutes, universities, commissions all over Rome. No one takes notice of where anyone comes from and many obscure offices are perpetually understaffed. While you at the Vatican look down your patrician noses at them, they form the invisible spine and backbone of the Church. Besides, you know Rome, your papers will not be routinely scrutinized, who has the time? Most employers won't look too closely, they'll be happy for an extra pair of hands."

"But I have no contacts outside the Vatican. You are right, I had no time for them and they led nowhere I considered forward. I can't use my own name, and I can't use the documents I entered Italy with."

"I, however, was never part of the Church elite. There are more good clerics there than you realize, many of whom are interested in the Beguines, in the charismatic approach. Unlike you, I left my orders behind, but I did not burn my bridges. I am making inquiries, very subtle inquiries. Documents are a problem, of course, but not an insurmountable one. Mostly you need a few letters of introduction, which can easily be obtained. Perhaps you will feel less an exile in Rome. Perhaps you will feel better if you can at least see the sharks in the water even if you no longer swim with them."

We did not speak of it again for a few weeks and life went on as though a scirocco blew each moment into the next, as though the moments tumbled after one another toward the confusion of the future. But I began to long for Rome and the longing overtook my fear, overtook my loneliness, overtook the contentment I felt in the work and the life.

One day Dominic said, "Your walls are still the work of a madman, the results of will and, I think, lust remembered. But they improve. I don't think you are destined for the brotherhood of masons, but there is a chance your walls will stand."

"Your praise fills me with pride."

"It is no longer the wall of a scholar. Not yet the work of an Egyptian, to be sure."

"I am the product of a misspent life."

"Probably a few of them."

"At least."

"Have I told you that masonry is a form of divination, like reading tea leaves?" Poncarelli could stand immobile in front of a wall as though he were stone himself.

"No."

"A sure form of divination. Past, present, future."

"What do you see in this wall?"

"The beast of your dreams."

CHAPTER
FORTY-THREE

On a clear bright afternoon after a rain, Dominic dragged me away from the primitive cement mixer. "Come. Tonight we will eat like the *padrone*." Behind the house was a massive stone outcropping. We scaled it and found ourselves in a small copse of chestnut trees. Poncarelli began to search. "There, and there. Look." On the ground, on the soft floor of the forest, were small patches of white and brown mushrooms. Poncarelli sank to his knees and, inspecting each carefully, began to pick them and put them into a cloth bag. I started to help him. "Careful, Gabriel. That one will kill you, and that other one will make you sick." When the bag was about half full, he stopped. "Enough." And we started back down the hill.

When we got back to our house, he built a fire in the fireplace. I got a long string of sausage from the refrigerator and a bottle of wine. In about twenty minutes the fire was ready. I put the sausages on the grill and opened the wine. With satisfaction, we watched them sizzle and sputter. Dominic went to the sink and washed the *fungi*, giving them one last inspection. He returned to the fire with the mushrooms and a loaf of bread.

"They won't kill us, will they?" I asked.

"If we die, my friend, we will die together."

"Very comforting."

"I was raised by a *nonna abruzzesa*. The best mycologists in the world. Trust me."

When the sausages were only a few minutes from being cooked, he put the mushrooms on the fire. He turned them once and a minute later we were eating them and the sausage, washing it all down with an Umbrian red wine.

We didn't speak for a while. The mushrooms tasted of earth and sky, of rain and the bright sunshine after rain.

"Dominic," I said, "I still don't understand. I see, with a kind of envy, how this is your place in the world. You say you're a peasant, and you take pleasure in this life in ways I appreciate but could never fully share. But you were also once a priest, even though I no longer see the priest in you. How did you arrive, finally, where you belong?"

Poncarelli shrugged and sighed. "In the Berkeley of 1965, I was just a parish priest. In the flats, in the ghetto. I had an old conservative pastor, half out of it, thinking the parish was still Irish or Italian, still thinking of the collection plate and the building plan. I was young and it was after Vatican II, of course, and we tried to make the liturgy relevant. I would wear dashiki vestments and have Dixieland jazz processions and try to say things from the pulpit against racism. Gabriel, just the obvious. I did not think of myself as a firebrand or a reformer. But my parish wasn't Irish or Italian, it was becoming more and more black. These people couldn't find decent employment, couldn't buy houses and yet their sons were getting drafted, going to Vietnam, and dying.

"Oh, I marched and listened to King, and heard him say that the civil rights movement was tied to the antiwar movement. Then he was killed and that made me more militant. I studied the draft regulations and counseled the young men of my parish on how to avoid the draft. Not a firebrand. I didn't get arrested, but I marched and I preached and tried to tend my flock." Poncarelli got up and moved the grill aside and put a large log on the fire. Then he took his place, lit a cigar, and continued.

"So I was summoned one night by the pastor, a Monsignor Kineally. He was half in the bag, he was not a brave man, and he said I had come to the attention of the diocese and I would have to stop these extrapriestly activities. Of course I protested and, of course, he deferred to the authority of the bishop. There was a big flap that year about the authority of the bishop. My bishop made it plain that no priest could espouse ideas not held by his bishop. No individual conscience, the will of the bishop, period. I made a few more attempts, got a few more reprimands, had to go to a few dreadful retreats."

"Pope Paul VI trying to close the Vatican doors and windows after John XXIII," I interjected.

"Exactly. The beginning of the end of the American Church. The beginning of the end, at least, for my priesthood. I didn't know it at the time, of course. I still marched but not in priestly garb. One by one my friends, all dedicated priests, left to get married, had nervous breakdowns, became drunks. I was headed in one of those directions, perhaps all three, when one Sunday afternoon I was wandering drunk and bored through the radio stations and by chance heard a talk given by Alan Watts. He was talking about eastern religions and about Zen, and something just clicked. I went to hear him, visited him on his houseboat in Sausalito, sat at his feet. He had one of the most beautiful voices I have ever heard, full of sadness, consciousness of his own edge, a whiskeyed sweetness, and a no-bullshit crankiness that was unique."

"So I studied the eastern arts—Zen, of course; did Vipassana, hung out at Esalen. Sufi stories, Swami Muktananda, even, I confess, Ragneesh. I remember once, Muktananda started a lecture, 'You can speak of God, or you can speak of consciousness; there is no difference.' That set me to thinking. In the seminary, of course, other religions, even Judaism, were ignored or scoffed at. Even our own mystical tradition—but you know all this." He put another log on the fire, went into the kitchen, and came back with a bottle of grappa and two small glasses.

"I delved," he continued." "John of the Cross, St. Francis, the monk Gregorianus. I was thorough. But the ache could not be stopped by scholarship. As we have discussed before, so many mystics were also involved with stopping very real carnage, only to have the hierarchy turn on them. I marched and counseled in Roman collar again. I wrote letters condemning the stance of my bishop, I defied my pastor. Finally I was invited, for want of a stronger word, to apply for a leave of absence from the priesthood. I refused. I became something of a hippie priest, working with runaway kids and speed burnouts on the avenue. I took psych classes at Berkeley, joined the SDS, even wore tie-dye vestments on occasion. Finally, the good bishop gave me a leave of absence, a one-way ticket to a monastery in Padua, and a lecture that still makes my ears ring. He was not a nice man.

"For some reason, I went. It was winter and I froze. But Padua was beautiful and I fell in love with Italy, and discovered that the monastery had a marvelous library with volumes dating back to the early Renaissance. Pico della Mirandola, who claimed to know everything and probably did. Ficino, who was Cosimo's translator; not only Plato, Aristotle, but also Hermes Trismegistus who got your friend Bruno in such trouble. My fellow monks gave me a wide berth. I had a wild angry look and no manners. I ignored their rules. I fled after Mass in the morning to the sacrosanct silence of the library with a loaf of bread and half a salami, and read all day. It took me six months but I found what I was looking for. The Beguines, the pure voices of poetry and mysticism. The ecstatic tradition of the Church, unheralded and unknown for centuries.

"For some reason, I wanted a practice that was still inside the Church. I just couldn't accept all the eastern chants and incantations. Even Zen left me a little cold. So I was happy to find my own tradition.

"Of course, I proselytized. In a few months, I had the monks rocking. Our liturgy was the talk of Padua. Ecstasy. A direct experience of God. Ah, but we neglected a few monastery rules here and there and I was singled out for censure and my old bishop had me back on his doorstep. But I had found myself and I had found God. The old drunk couldn't believe the sweetness of my smile, the gentleness of my nature. He sent me to the suburbs. Well, I hadn't changed that much. Orinda was only a few minutes from Berkeley. I volunteered at the free clinic, bringing kids down from acid, watching a growing procession of homeless troop through our offices, many of them Vietnam veterans. I turned them on to my ecstatic practices, ex-druggies, ex-Hare Krishnas, ex-soldiers. More grappa? This is really good, made by an old *contadino* in Tuscany. Hint of orange, taste it?

"The bishop was sick and old by that time, about five days older than God, we used to joke, and twice as mean. Hippie priests were not tolerated, not two-time losers. I had some relatives in Italy—"

"In the Abruzzi, right?" I took a sip of grappa, and winced at the strength of the liquor and the memory.

"Ah, Gabriel, you have reason to remember! A gaggle of my youthful supporters followed me there and you know the rest. I hear about my former associates from time to time. All the healthy priests are married and have five kids or are openly gay. Many of the priests who stayed were the ones we avoided, the loners with no agenda, who ended up cruising for altar boys. The last time I heard, half the parish churches were closed or in serious trouble. A sad history. They drove us away, the priests with consciences. Now they don't have the brains to understand the results. I have no sympathy."

"Why aren't you married with five kids?"

"I think I told you once. I loved being a priest, witnessing for God. By the time I'd had my fill of it, I was too old and set in my ways. What would a woman want with an old priest?"

"I told you about Jean."

"Yes, but you are a little younger and you were lucky. I must admit I never saw you as that vulnerable. She must be an extraordinary woman."

"She is. But I, too, think I have the stamp burned too deep in me. So much happened so fast. She knew I would run with her but in the end, in the end, I would still be a priest and she would have lost everything. I couldn't ask it of her, and she would never have accepted it."

"You miss her."

"Yes. I know she is better off without a priest only half out of orders . . . but still, I wonder."

"Of course. They shouldn't have . . . ah, the grappa is almost gone. I must renew my acquaintance. In the meantime, I am tired, Gabriel. *Buona notte.*"

"*Et cum spiritu tuo.*" Our laughter made a hollow echo against the stone of the walls.

CHAPTER
FORTY-FOUR

The scirocco stopped blowing and the heat of the day seared us as we worked. I meditated. I walked the hills on old trails the Romans had built, trying to find the essence of Francis, stumbling each time into traps set by my personality. I had changed. Many illusions had been stripped away with my ambitions. Dominic pointed out to me over and over that to be consumed with failure was still to be consumed with ambition, but I could not shake the feelings. The old mask had cracked, had been left on a beach thousands of miles away, but still I fought the same battles against the need to find a defining context on which to hang an identity, any identity.

Yet there was a sense of brotherhood with Camillo, Rigo, and Poncarelli, which was the bond of common purpose and work. The work was hard, but it was never without humor, never without song or talk of food. Good food, cheap wine, foul-smelling cigars, and endless conversation. The combination is uniquely Italian.

"Dominic, you didn't really answer me last night when I asked you what happened to the desire to be one with God, to be with God. Why did you abandon the Beguines?"

"I didn't abandon them, Gabriel. I am still trying to find that ecstasy, that point where my personality disappears and immensity begins. I came, I come close, so close, but then I tire of the forms, or forms become so important in themselves that they infect my meditation. The Beguines are important, a mystical link that exists in Christianity, but I couldn't, finally, rid myself of the romantic, of the courtly-love aspect of their quest. I tired of seeing God as the Beloved, tired of the whole anthropomorphic mess that went along with it."

"But what of transcendence, of that ecstasy? I think I felt it on the beach. My personality disappeared and I could see and hear so clearly and I knew what I had to do."

"But how long did it last?"

"The effects wear off so quickly. For a day, maybe two, objects were still defined in space, color was true and unfiltered. The sense that I knew what my life was about and that it made obvious sense disappeared almost immediately, and has never truly reappeared."

"Exactly. That has been my experience also, and I nearly despaired. I could live on that plane for a while, but when I came back, I still had to undergo the same pain, the same indecision, push against the same failings. Reality became a straitjacket, yet I could not control the ecstatic state, couldn't prolong it. Then I remembered that Muktananda, the old pervert, said that consciousness is God and God is consciousness."

"I remembered you said something about it the other night. Didn't Muktananda preach celibacy and then get caught in the sack with a young girl? I think I read about it. It was about the same time the head of the Zen Center, the first Anglo Zen master, got caught *in flagrante* with the wife of one of his followers."

"You see the pitfalls. Not just sex, but any number of things. These spiritual guides, these mystics, set out on a search, a real search for—what did your woman-friend call it?—higher states. And they work very hard, and achieve certain results, verifiable results."

"Verifiable but not quantifiable."

"Yes. These states are reached but no one is prepared for the toll it takes. So many who preach celibacy wish to take that sensual impulse and trade it for energy in these altered states. That sad aberration was probably behind the thinking of the early fathers. They tried to make one energy equal the other. But it seems that energy attaches itself and the more they tried to control it, the stronger it became."

"What are you saying, Dominic?"

"I'm saying that I had to give it up, the desire to live the ecstatic life. I couldn't maintain my everyday life. Being sent to Calabria changed me. You should have gone yourself. I learned that everyday life is the only path. After all, a path is simply putting one foot in front of the other. It is madness to succeed in ecstasy only to lose in reality. It's not acceptable. You had a big experience. It changed your life and I am glad for that. You are still left with the same personality. Witness the fact that you are still blind to the beauty of this place. Witness that you still wring your hands over what is better put into the past and forgotten. You are changed, Gabriel, but the fight is and always will be moment by moment. It is mean, sweat-stained work that daily grazes despair, but it is God, or all we have of God. We have never let ourselves know God the way modern scientists know him. We still think of an orderly universe of immutable laws, of crystal spheres. Yet we know now that it is a place of chaos and uncertainty, that every law holds in one place and not in another, that the universe incorporates the random, the inexplicable. That is the face of God, Gabriel. You have been infected with all the dualities. If you are not a success you are a failure; if not good, then evil; if not orderly, then chaotic."

"Are you saying there is no order, no immutable laws, like gravity or the speed of light?"

"That is not order, Gabriel, that is pattern. The universe tosses off these infinitely complex patterns which we conveniently reduce to a defining order."

"What the hell does that have to do with us? With this conversation?"

"Everything. If there are no convenient dualities, if there is no easily definable good or evil, then we are alone with the alone and all there is to hang on to is consciousness, the eternal unfolding of the pattern."

"Which is God?"

"Can there be another? By the way, I received a letter from Rome today. There might be a place opening up in an obscure library not attached to the Vatican. I understand it is quite interesting; it seems they have been cataloguing heretical or forbidden books for a few centuries. Quite a collection, always kept up to date. The assistant librarian had been there for a century or so himself. Died finally. They say his skin had turned to parchment and instead of blood they found vermilion. Right up your alley."

"Oh God."

"Ah, but it comes with an apartment near the Pantheon and a nice stipend and total invisibility to the world, even to the Vatican. The Vatican is forbidden to acknowledge its existence. The perfect rabbit hole."

"How soon?"

"Few things to tidy up. Papers, etc. You must finish the wall you are building, I am interested in what it augurs."

"Poncarelli, you are crazy."

"And if you stayed much longer, you would be too, as well as dead. I buy my foul-smelling cigars in Umbertide. My tobacconist says rather sinister *stranieri* have been asking questions."

Poncarelli made me stay at the house or the work site, no more trips to town, no more excursions. I finished my wall and prepared to leave. I stood in front of the wall I had built for a long time. For the first time I felt like an Italian mason. There was not a speck of mortar on me, not even on my shoes. There was a fine layer of sand and cement on my hands, but they were not caked with it. Camillo and Alfredo laughed and joked with me as they criticized my work. It was sound, the wall would stand. But there was something unbalanced about it. Built by someone in a hurry who had nowhere to go and couldn't wait to get there, someone who had chosen the stones carefully but with a kind of abstraction as if part of his mind were somewhere else.

194

It was almost as if the wall was forced out of someone who did not want to make a definite statement, someone who was more comfortable with rhetoric and obfuscation, someone who knew he would never enjoy it. It was built by someone against his will, someone who had spent too long a time doing things against his will until he knew no other way. The flash of death, like a photographer's strobe, illumined the moment and I cursed Poncarelli and his divination.

CHAPTER
FORTY-FIVE

It was a Wednesday and Poncarelli came home from the Umbertide market with a rabbit. I made a marinade of red wine, garlic, rosemary, and handful of dried herbs. That night we cooked it for a few hours until the wine had almost evaporated, and the meat had begun to come away from the bone. We ate the *coniglio* with roasted potatoes and a salad of wild greens.

I was to leave for Rome in a few days, and there was still so much to understand.

"When did the image of the devil, the Christian devil, first appear, Gabriel?"

"I never thought of it."

"Why not?" Poncarelli pushed his plate away and re-filled our glasses. "We seem to have always pictured the devil in the same way, the same features, height and weight. The devil is never blond, never obese. Always a tempter, a whisperer in ears, never badly dressed, come to think of it. Who was the first to depict him that way? Why the cloven hooves, the tail, the lascivious grin of the lecher? He always seems to enjoy watching others sin, to enjoy the resulting damnation."

"For instance, didn't the story of Job ever bother you? God willing to bet on Job with the devil like a scientific experiment. It may be an attempt to show how suffering is meant by the Almighty as a test of faith, but it's a little coldblooded if you ask me. Not only that, but Job wins, has his fields and animals and health restored. Makes you wonder."

I took my time answering, savoring the food like a

man worried about his next meal. "Not only that," I said, "but it makes all the pitfalls of life somehow the work of the devil, everything from mosquitoes to malaria."

"But Gabriel, that starts with Genesis and all the earthly paradise crap."

"But the devil is a snake. And he tempts Adam and Eve with knowledge of good and evil. That always struck me as strange. That the desire for consciousness *is* the evil. To be like a god. It reminds me of something I read once. In the creation story in the *Pimander* of Hermes Trismegistus, there is no original sin as such. Man chooses his nature of his own free will, and with that choice comes mortality and the rest. It was man's consciousness that was the fall, and the fall was a *result* not a punishment."

"What about the temptation by Eve?" Poncarelli had a puzzled look on his face, as if he was working out a problem.

"That was always bothersome too, wasn't it?" I continued. "No, in this version, man chooses his nature, chooses consciousness, and this choice meant a loss of corporeal immortality, meant that he would be tied to the rack of time, to the cycles of death and rebirth and to final death with only the dimmest notion of his spiritual ancestry."

"What about evil in this version, Gabriel? We are so tied to it, how can we imagine the fall without it?" Poncarelli stopped speaking suddenly and gestured to me at the same time to be silent. I listened. I heard what I thought to be muffled voices at some distance from the house. We turned out the lights and stood on the loggia, concealed by a stone pillar. We heard what seemed to be large animals moving about in the brush. This was not unusual; in the woods that nearly circled the house were wild boar, which often moved through the undergrowth at night. Yet the sounds formed a pattern of movement back and forth across the hill behind the house. Poncarelli and I had often hunted mushrooms along the trails used by boar hunters and mushroom hunters. The hills were a labyrinth of trails, some of them rumored to be part of an old Roman road. We strained to hear, but the sounds stopped.

Then they started again, moving swiftly away from the house and down the road. We heard boots crush on gravel. A car sputtered to life and started down the road. Only when it rounded the first curve did its lights flare up against the hillside.

Poncarelli, a look of apprehension and anger replacing confusion, turned and I turned with him to see the first flames leap up out of the undergrowth and begin to follow the line of gasoline that had been spread a few yards from the house. We ran through the house, throwing open windows as we went, and saw the flames lick at the trees and then the trees caught and the blaze rushed up the trees and began to crown from one to the other. We knew it would only be moments before we were engulfed in flames. I threw a few clothes into a canvas bag, and went to find Poncarelli. We had to shout at each other to make ourselves heard over the roar of the flames. Then we heard the natural-gas tank blow and it sounded as though someone had ignited a bomb. Dominic and I realized simultaneously that only one possibility was left to us.

We threw open the heavy double doors at the front of the house and in a moment were down the stone stairs and racing toward the widest path, the ancient road. But the fire raged around us, creating its own windstorm as it moved. I ran wildly, Poncarelli a few steps ahead, his huge chest heaving with exertion. At times we were a few yards ahead of the storm, at times it flanked us. We choked and coughed but we ran. Soon the path narrowed and we could barely see the way and we ran on instinct, on memory, on panic, and then only with desperation. I have heard it described but had never experienced it, that feeling when the will and muscles are exhausted and yet one continues, blinded and scorched, cinders falling on our clothes and almost catching before we outran them.

We crossed a small stream, little more than a trickle at that time of year. We paused for a moment to roll in the tepid water. I looked at Dominic and he looked back and I knew that he saw what I saw, the wild, mad-eyed, cornered animal dragging his body through an inferno. It was then I understood the final message of my dreams. The flight that carried my body and spirit was not toward damnation but salvation. Then we were running again, stumbling, picking each other up and moving on. Sweat-blind, scorched, we rushed forward toward a wide, dark expanse with one bright star that seemed to draw us into its protection. A few minutes of agony and we reached the clearing. We stood and looked back at the devastation behind us. In the distance we could hear sirens; ahead of us a mile up a crushed rock road lay Preggio, a small but impregnable village of about thirty families that had survived plagues, earthquakes, blight, famine, and war, and would survive this fire, would survive even the two men who entered its sanctuary, hanging on to each other like two drunks, alternating between laughter and tears, coughing and ragged, but alive.

Poncarelli and I staggered toward a small restaurant. There were people in the streets and they looked at us with alarm. A few recognized us and moved to support us. They were men from the village who worked as masons or farmed small tobacco farms in the valley below.

They rang the bell and the proprietress appeared tying her apron. She was the grandmother of the family and had the lively seriousness and gentle temperament of most Italians. She brought water-soaked towels and a carafe of water and brandy.

"*Male, male, male,*" she whispered as she helped us clean ourselves, helped clean the deep scratches and the burns, which were sometimes in the shape of oak leaves. We drank some brandy and a kind of calm overtook us, a silence. We had seen the naked look of animals, had behaved with their instinct and their will. This would always be our bond, our totem. In the silence I felt we knew that this was consciousness also, that beneath the mason, the scholar, the priest is that which lives deep in the forest, wild and untamable.

CHAPTER FORTY-SIX

We became unashamedly drunk. Those who had remained with us shook their heads at us and drank also. There were questions in their glances, but they had too much gentility to ask them and we had too much to hide to answer. Just before dawn two of the men took us to an empty house, pointed us to a bed, and left us there.

I slept until early afternoon, until I could no longer bear the sunlight. I lay there a while, unable to believe how much every muscle and joint ached, only surpassed by how much my head ached. I had just finished dressing when Poncarelli returned, looking old and battered.

"We must move quickly."

"Where?"

"Just follow me."

He turned and climbed down the stairs, holding on to the thin wooden handrail for support. In his other hand was a small rucksack. A truck waited outside with its motor running. Dominic turned to me. There were tears in his eyes. "This will take you to Chiusa. There is a train to Rome." He gestured to the rucksack. "In here are all the papers you need."

"Dominic, what are you going to do? It's not safe for you either."

"No. It is you they are after. I will work and everything will be the way it was before. I think this is perhaps my place and I will piss off the perimeters of it like a wolf, like a wolf." He smiled and helped me into the back of the truck where there was a place for me among the bales of tobacco.

I sat down heavily and looked about. A canvas flap closed and I was plunged into darkness. *Out of the depths I cry to you . . . Hear my prayer.* I fumbled with the rucksack and felt inside. Under the packet of papers and a thick envelope that almost filled the sack were half a loaf of bread, a hunk of *parmigiana*, and a bottle of wine. The flap opened an hour later and I was at the train station at Chiusa. I bought a ticket and took my place on the train in a deserted car. I looked again inside the sack. Poncarelli had thought to take the manuscript from the kitchen table on our way out. He must have sheltered it with his body as we ran.

CHAPTER
FORTY-SEVEN

I fell into this library as if into a coma. The letters and documents Poncarelli had put together for me were enough. The priest, a Father Selvaggio who oversaw the library, was almost ninety himself and was overjoyed just to find a priest who knew something about ancient books.

"Of course, most of the books in this library are heretical works." Father Selvaggio almost giggled. "We collect whatever our budget allows. But we have copies of the profane masterpieces also. Oh, many volumes. And apocrypha, the gnostic gospels, the occult, satanic and demonic, plus arcana, cabala, Jewish and Christian. The Vatican pretends we don't exist, but they request books nonetheless. We send them by courier, all very secret. You would expect their interest would be mostly in the gnostic, but I can assure you it is quite eclectic. Your duties will not be altogether strenuous. I am, I am proud to say, almost ninety. I have worked here for seventy-five years. You see, we librarians outlive even symphony conductors.

"I trust your apartment is satisfactory?" he asked.

"It is more than adequate, perhaps a little spartan."

"Oh yes," he said with a dry laugh, "spartan. But no, Father, not spartan. It is not a gymnasium, naked girls and boys covered with olive oil doing martial exercises. No indeed. It is spare, perhaps hermitic. But no, nothing in Rome is exactly hermitic, lacking the oriental touch, you see. Let's leave it at spare. Spare is very good."

The conversation went on, taking abrupt turns and winding back on itself. Father Selvaggio was an ancient patrician, tall and thin. His posture was erect and he had perhaps the most perfect example of a Roman nose I had ever seen. His cassocks were always perfectly tailored and spotless, their cuffs never frayed. He never sweated, coughed, or exhibited an emotion other than self-absorbed amusement. He read Latin, of course, but also Greek, Russian, Chinese, Arabic, and Aramaic, and he could decipher hieroglyphics and the rudiments of Sumerian cuneiform. He seemed to have read everything from Assyrian battle records to the Marquis de Sade. I never saw him without a book. In fact there were always stacks of books on his desk.

The library itself looked like all libraries. Three floors of stacks, rows and rows of books, some of them parchment bound in leather, some in manuscript form. There were books cross-referenced with inquisitorial testimony. A giant encyclopedia of heresies covered one wall. It was intriguing, awesome. It was a nightmare.

I often replayed the night I ran through the burning woods; like my dreams, the last years had seemed a run through fire, a persistent danger pushing the blood through my veins. I had seen myself slowly stripped of all comfort, all false morality, had broken all vows, had been forced to survive on instinct only to find myself trapped again in the airless cloister of Holy Orders. There have been whole days I did nothing but relive every moment with Jean, where I went over each experience again and again, trying desperately to understand.

My duties were irregular and sporadic. Sometimes I had to feign busyness, filling boxes with books requested by some agency of the Church, or uncrating new acquisitions which had come to this place by diverse and unchartable routes. Other times, I found a quiet place to read and to write or meditate. Father Selvaggio seemed to float slowly by, always with a book under his arm and a look of wry amusement on his face. He never expected more from me or less, as long as my cassock was clean and I was reasonably sober. For some reason, ever since that night in the Umbrian forest, I was.

I confess (confession comes easier without guilt) it was only the threat of discovery that kept me going, kept me from disintegration. First the threat, then this confession, this apology which has outgrown its first two envelopes and threatens to grow larger than the third. I ran across a Sufi story in the Islamic section about a Sufi who is called before the sultan and told under pain of execution to share proof of his special powers. "I see devils under the earth and angels in the heavens," he shouted. The sultan was astonished and impressed. "How did you do that?" he queried. "Fear is all you need," replied the Sufi.

My demons are real, of course, and fear keeps them close. Until quite recently, they were invisible. Now as the end draws near, fear keeps them in sharp relief. The angels, however, have kept their distance. A very polite distance. In a world that seems to dissolve before my eyes into terror and chaos, it seems the angels have kept an increasing distance. I imagine them sometimes, cowering in heaven, afraid of venturing too close to the civil wars and famines and plagues that have befallen us. Angels are no fools.

When I was a child, and expected to think as a child, I was told that each of us has a guardian angel, perhaps only to offset the terror of having the devil in one ear always tempting toward damnation. It was a comfort, this guardian. But when I began to read history, I wondered why they disappeared at the first sign of real trouble. What happened to the angels of the Armenians, Cambodians, Vietnamese, the Tamils, Somalis, Jews, Croatians? Even the Irish seem severely lacking in guardians. Anyway, I had given up long ago on any sense of a guardian, and had even stopped feeling lonely as a consequence.

When I asked Father Selvaggio, just to pass the time

one afternoon, he wheezed and said, "All the fault of misdating. Saint Dionysus in a vision saw all the choirs of angels, was taught their hierarchy, you know, Thrones, Dominions, Powers, or is it the other way around? Now he was said to be contemporaneous with the biblical authors, a few thousand years before Christ, which for some reason would make him more believable. The medieval mind worshiped the ancients. Pity, I was born too late. Be that as it may, the older the better, the more authentic. So, if you were Moses you could do no wrong. Of course, you have the Renaissance to thank also. They rediscovered all the old learning, most of it copied and kept who knows where. So we must forgive them if they slipped up on a few dates. Saint Dionysus indeed. After everyone had bought it, Throne by Domination, it was discovered the manuscript had been created in the second century Anno Domini. Much less worthy of reverence, of course. Ah, but then I think we still revere the Shroud of Turin. No one would think of using it to wrap fish in the Campo dei Fiori, now would they? Or the blood of San Gennaro, a pretty mystery, that. I just catalogued all the papers on it. It seems the liquefying blood could be faked with materials known to our early Fathers of the Church, who perhaps thought the faith of the faithful would benefit from fresh miracles. They fetched a pretty price. If you assembled all the relics of the True Cross, wouldn't you own a lumberyard, my friend? Guardian angels. The wings of Selvaggio's angel must be in sorry shape by now. Retire the wretch, I say! He's earned a rest."

The afternoon shadows had long since gathered us into gloom before he finished by reminding me that St. Louis of France had once paid a king's ransom, a king's ransom literally, for what purported to be the crown of thorns, a nail from the cross, and a feather from the wings of the Archangel Gabriel. "Faith, Father, is something we have in spite of our own history, not because of it."

CHAPTER
FORTY-EIGHT

One day I was walking across the Piazza Farnese when I heard someone call a name behind me. Finally there was a tug at my sleeve. "Father Wolfe, don't you know your own name?" I froze. It was Jenny.

"You said if I was ever in Rome to look you up. Well, you are harder to find than the city of Andocentyn, and that's a myth. Nobody here has ever heard of you. Had to find you by accident."

I kissed her on both cheeks.

"You look like you've seen a ghost," she said. "Do I look like a ghost? Am I happy to see you. Rome is amazing, but the men! I'm worn out from looking mean. Don't have no mean left. Walking down the street smiling at nobody, what kind of way is that?" She was wearing skintight jeans and a silk shirt. Her hair was tied up with a bright scarf and she wore huge gold hoop earrings.

"I know what you're thinking, but my Mother Teresa outfit is at the cleaners."

"You look wonderful."

"Wish I could say the same for you. You live in a cave? You are pale and sad-looking. You headed for that trattoria? Well, I'm buying."

We ate *fritto misto*, veal chops with deep-fried sage, and shared a bottle of wine. She made it look easy, filling in the gaps in the conversation, trying to set me at ease, talking about her work, what had happened to her since the crop circles. Somehow she knew not to ask questions, and while she was animated I could see disappointment in her eyes.

"The crop circles were a bust, Padre. Everything went to hell after you left. I cried on Father Dunstan's shoulder a few times and that only embarrassed both of us. Don't know what you pulled but St. Jerold's was left to crumble on its own for a while. Two dudes say they did all the circles after a few pints and the papers picked it up worldwide. No one investigated much, like how did they do about three thousand circles and all that. I wrote a paper on them, which no one will touch now, so apart from a disaster it was a disaster. Kicked around here and there trying to trace the Druids to an exiled clan of Pelasgians, translated a few Druidic poems, going back and forth to the south of France. It all gave me a headache."

"What brings you to Rome?"

"I got a small grant to study the secret rites of the Vestals, if you can believe that. Some rich bored feminists, who knows?"

"I might be able to help you . . . I have some erudite contacts."

"You're no *end* of surprises. I was beginning to wonder if you were a figment of my imagination. But you're weirder than I can make up so you must be real. Lunch is on me, or on the foundation, bless their souls. If you dig anything up, I'm in Trastevere, here's my number. You got a phone?"

"Not exactly."

"I suspected as much."

I said good-bye hurriedly and left. I walked back to the library by every back street I knew. Rome is an impossible place to follow someone, an unplanned labyrinth. I almost panicked. I started at any figure behind me. I tried to tell myself it was only paranoia, but if an angel could stumble on me . . . Fear is all you need. When I reached the sanctuary of the library I almost genuflected with relief. I was sweating, panting.

Father Selvaggio looked up from a huge book, a medieval occult recipe book we had just received from the estate of an old count who dabbled in sorcery. "We are not that busy, Father, no need to run back."

CHAPTER
FORTY-NINE

What saves one in difficulty? So many times, in hind-
sight, I should have despaired, should have lost hope
and will completely. But it is never that simple. To lose
hope is such a hopeful act, after all. The thought that
there is no combination of circumstances that offers redemption begs the central question, begs the need to
question, to make contact, to understand another and
be understood in turn. The hopeless are such optimists.

I had no such optimism and no real hope. Yet I awakened each morning with the sense that something might
conceivably happen to change the sentence of the Fates,
to restart the wheel. At the same time, each pulse beat
brought death one diastolic moment closer. I felt what
the condemned feel without the certainty of the exact
moment. There is hope in knowing the final moment.
Even behind the growing panic must be the consciousness that finality approaches. Even the nihilists fall into
the ranks of the optimists. To believe that death is the
end of suffering, the end of all consequences, is such a
comforting notion.

I have lived in the shadow of the Christian heaven
and hell and have ceased to take the quaint notions of
either very seriously. That there is a universal system,
a universal bureaucracy that somehow sorts the good
from the bad, that takes account of all private and public acts, intentions, thoughts, and is capable and com-
petent to judge these matters—the idea is ludicrous.
That other bureaucracies preside over endless bliss or
torment is equally ludicrous. Yet who is to say that no

mechanism exists, however strange and arbitrary, that ensures some kind of afterlife, either some means of shoehorning life energy, cleansed of memory and ego, into another frail body for one more go-round, or perhaps simply a disembodied entity floating in universal memory. Who can be so sure based on little or no reliable evidence? What I understand of the universe leads me to distrust deeply the notion of an orderly and just transition into the beyond. The universe is filled with dust and stars and planets without number, without apparent order, a place capable of appalling violence as well as vast reaches of nothingness. And I don't trust it.

I can forgive our Fathers their quaint visions, based on what? A feverish and surreal Book of Revelation? Why not treat the paintings of Hieronymus Bosch as snapshots? Anyway, they only had the witness of their unaided senses and their collective fears on which to base their cosmology. We have more sophisticated devices and our collective fears on which to base ours and our cosmology has advanced little because our scientifically enhanced senses have not unclouded a vision of reality so obscured by fear.

I can speak clearly because my fears are intertwined with the knowledge of my death. To be conscious of it is to already begin to experience it. In my meditations, I stab at the curtain again and again and each time I understand more and more about the universe, which serves to increase my uncertainty and decrease my desire to place myself in its care.

And so I hide and play the game, play it a little recklessly, but with the knowledge of the confirmed realist; no matter what my belief about what awaits me, it does not serve my interests to speed the inexorable process.

Which is why I found myself, a few days later, at Jenny's doorstep with a small stack of books about the Vestal Virgins under my arm.

"I have a confession to make," I began.
"I thought you heard them, not made them."

"I have little experience with either."

And then, as though the burden had suddenly become intolerable, I told her the story of Father Wolfe and what had happened since. I paced the rapidly darkening apartment. I searched her face for the courage to continue. I would fall silent and stare out the window at trees, the faintest breath of the Ponentino stirring through them. I would then find the thread of my story and continue. It felt at times I was telling a story I had learned, and in some ways it was. Jenny sat composed and distant, confronted suddenly by a stranger with a strange and tortured story. She listened without moving. She didn't rise to turn on a lamp, she didn't interrupt. I was left alone with my story.

Echoes from the past resonated in my imagination. Perhaps I was trying to explain my nature, or deduce what must be my nature from the tale I told. I stood silently at the window. The bar downstairs was coming to life. Cars were parked three deep and the sounds of laughter rang through the trees like accusations. She tried to sound brave, but her voice broke with anger. "For all these months I was so worried. I tried to pray, Padre, but no one ever taught me how. It seemed so real, you were so dignified in your exile, hard to believe it was all for show, all a lie."

"All the lies have caught up with me, Jenny. Now the exile is real. Father Wolfe was a little ahead of himself."

She came over and stood next to me and together we looked out over Trastevere, the glow from the restaurants, the lighted fountains, the timeless monuments attesting to life in all its complex mystery, the promises made and broken, the whispered secrets of the past just out of earshot. I could smell the perfume of her dark hair and longed for the balm of her absolution.

"Damn you. It's not that easy." She turned to look at me, angry tears welling in her. "Something passed between me and someone who doesn't exist. It hurts. Father Wolfe was real to me. And it was all a lie. That's not how I live my life. That's not what *I* do to friends, and nobody ever taught *me* right from wrong. You lived next to something your whole life and it never touched you. How do you explain that?"

I wanted to tell her that my life had been a series of disguises. I wanted to comfort her, to defend the indefensible pattern of my life. I remained silent, letting the light from the rooftops, the light from the Fontana on the Gianicolo, wash over us.

Jenny smiled a tight, mirthless smile, "I liked you better as Father Wolfe."

"I liked me better as Father Wolfe."

"But he was a lie."

"Yes, but I miss him. If only because you liked him."

"And I'm not at all sure I like you. You're too sad and confused. Defeated by your victories. Too comfortable in your complexity."

"The mouths of babes."

"What?"

"Nothing. It is late."

Jenny's head tilted a little to the side. I left quickly, sadness burning much brighter in my heart than virtue ever could.

The night was warm and it was early by Roman standards. I turned toward the Piazza Trilussa and the Tiber, and crossed the Ponte Sisto. But I had no desire to confront Bruno this night, so I turned right and crossed over into the old Jewish quarter. Crowds of youths stood talking as others slowly circled them on Vespas. I dove into a side street to avoid their boisterous optimism, and the winding medieval gloom of the ancient ghetto fed my mood. Time-blackened buildings loomed on either side with decorated cornices supported by griffins and lions with gaping mouths. These streets were utterly deserted and seemed filled with a cabalistic silence that hid its wisdom in shadow, yet the protection of that magic was powerless against the modernist swagger of the Fascist. I stopped again at a small bar on the Via Delfini for a brandy. The bar was owned by an old-style Communist and, like the heraldic beasts and griffins of that quarter, his walls sprouted busts of Stalin and a woven Chinese tapestry of Lenin's face. There was Sandino glowering under his huge hat, and a smiling youthful Che chomping on a cigar. There was Gramsci, and Gorbachev, and a host of Italian Communist leaders. I sipped a brandy and wondered whether the harsh taste of remorse and spurned ardor could ever be dissolved in alcohol. Whatever alchemy was required, I was willing to learn.

An overcoated figure crossed in front of the window, which was almost entirely obscured by invitations to rallies, the shouts of which had long since ceased to echo down from the Campidoglio. I was occupied and preoccupied with my own past. At that moment, it was a seamless gray whole with a few ragged holes where someone else's emotion had burned through and left frayed and singed areas that rendered the whole useless. What could I ever, even as Father Wolfe, have offered to match her innocence and freshness?

The shadow crossed the window again. The proprietor, a graying man with a mirthless smile beneath perpetually amused eyes, poured me another brandy without being asked. I was the prelate of sadness, the only parish I would ever call my own.

The shadow passed a third time and there was a harsh ringing in my ears, like a messenger leaning on a bell in the middle of the night. My hands felt cold around the glass and the small flame of warmth and forgetfulness engendered by the whiskey vanished.

Dominic! The time has come to post the packages! The ancient stone streets are a labyrinth, a labyrinth my worn black shoes know perfectly. I was the brother of every Jew hunted in these streets, the brother of all those haunted by the patriarchal shadow of the Vatican. How many, at the mercy of how many tyrants, felt as I then felt? As I paid at the small register by the door, I whispered *Morituri te salutamus*. The small man behind the counter looked up quizzically and smiled.

Dominic, do not think that I fled that night, that I passed through the safety of that comradely door with any hopeful illusions. It was a reflex, like taking the next breath. Even the despairing take one more breath, then another, not with hope but perhaps abandoning themselves to the mechanistic world of reflex action, like a man falling who takes no action to break the fall through space. But how alive the reflexes are! What a great general fear is, even to the hopeless. It is with this abandon I crossed the threshold, turned right in the darkness of the Delfini, and set out with long strides down the small hill toward the Piazza Mattei.

CHAPTER
FIFTY

I sensed his presence behind me, behind me at least six or seven doorways. By now it was midnight and there was no sound. The police car that keeps its lonely watch at the end of the Delfini had disappeared. He was in no hurry and he seemed to know these streets. All the metal doors were rolled down and the even more forbidding ancient wooden doors were locked against the night. Life went on happily behind them. A wonderful dinner, a small cup of coffee, a little grappa perhaps. I could hear a few bars of Tosca as I fled, then Sinatra; a saxophone squealed as I turned back toward the Portico d'Ottavia and the Teatro Marcello. The crowd had thinned until only a Vespa or two made heedless circles in the wide street. I rushed between them and on toward the immense synagogue with its automatic eyes scanning the horizon for trouble. I turned right and then left, crossed the Via Arenula and headed for the Campo dei Fiori. I followed the sound of Ray Charles singing "Georgia on My Mind" and found a *vineria* where the door opening was like the mouth of a cave. Wine bottles lined shelves that reached the vaulted ceiling. A few self-involved drunks milled around the bar waiting for the right foreign woman to appear and turned back to the bar when I entered. I ordered a beer *della spina* and moved toward the corner where I could look as if I was inspecting the vintages and keep my eye on the door.

The man who had been following me did not appear. I watched and sipped, trying to decide between the

1982 Barolo and a 1984 Brunello. I was entranced by the choice, by the idea that there were such human and comforting choices to be made, as though I was involved in little more than a late night walk through the familiar streets.

"*Buona sera*, Father D'Amato, if that is the correct phrase."

I started at the voice, turned and found Sir Henry Throckmorton smiling at me. He wore a dark suit and an overcoat and had a glass of red wine in his left hand. His smile was full of malicious and darkly triumphant glints that would have looked natural on a satyr.

"Yes. *Buona sera.*"

"You have not been easy to find. Hiding in Rome was a brilliant ploy. The place is positively crawling with obscure clerics doing suitably obscure things. We found you quite by accident, really. A chap heard someone call out to a Father Wolfe and a little bell jingled in his otherwise worthless anatomy."

I nodded. And a chill settled in my bones that has never left.

"You ran out on your duties, Father. Hell of a row. Had the devil to pay and that won't do for a prince of the Church. The very devil splashing scandal over the wires. A false bishop consorting and cavorting in sunny California. Bit of a kiss and tell and hit the road.

"Ah, but didn't you give them tantalizing little grapes about your work, what you might have heard in the vast halls? Enough to show your superiors what you know, and enough to let them know you know much more. The devil to pay.

"And of course the Virgin fiasco, that hurt more, much more. The Vatican is more than good at riding out the odd scandal. They've had more practice than the British royalty, which is considerable. Old money and a little pomp acquire their own dignity, just about all the dignity left in the world. If you gild the edges with gold, who will care to look much deeper? A few investigators. The likes of you and them have been after me for years. It has cost me too. A million pounds you have cost me alone. But it is only the cost of doing business, Father. I won't worry until they nail old Licio Gelli and his crowd. But the Virgin business. That hurts in all the wrong places. Delicate balances. As you well know. Delicate balances. Does the Vatican want the world to know it regularly dispatches its best and brightest to clamp a hand over the mouths of the faithful? No, Father, it does not. Does the Vatican want one of its own having his own vision and splashing it across the world's airwaves? No, it does not. Does your fat monsignor want to deal with the bloody Americans who don't go to church anyway, who follow their own bloody rules? Who listen to your lot telling them to pray for peace and love, while they close the churches and the schools and try to find priests who will keep their mouths shut and not bugger each other. I don't have to tell you how close to anarchy it is over there, almost worse than schism. And the likes of you.

"Mary covens springing up all over. My God." Sweat glistened on his brow. He kept his voice low but poisonous and threatening.

I kept my own voice low and flat. "What has this to do with you or me any longer? I am out of the picture, no threat to anyone."

"Are you now? Who can be sure about you? Can we just let all the likes of you wander around talking to journalists? Indeed. There's no bloody Inquisition to keep the faithful in line. Not like the old days. Just a few organizations like mine. Doing the work of God. Laymen with a certain bit of influence going to places and doing things that might dirty the soutanes of the clerics."

"Apparitions of the Virgin can't threaten anyone. If anything, they bring the faithful back into the Church."

"It's gotten out of hand, out of the papal control. Costing millions, maybe billions in lost revenues. Everyone his own church, pick and choose. Abortion, birth control, papal infallibility. Up for grabs. Worse than an invasion of Vandals, worse than the cold war. Fighting the godless held it together for fifty years. Us against them. The holy against the infidel. Now no one can even get it together to fight Islam. And we make bloody pals with the Jews. Then all these women talking to Mary. Got to stop it somewhere. Even the Italians won't listen to the pope anymore."

"Perhaps he should change his message."

"He's the pope only as long as he *won't* change the message."

I was tired and talking to Throckmorton was like talking to a petulant and malicious child. He wasn't even looking at me. His eyes had wandered up and he looked beyond me at a private battlefield, at a battle the outcome of which he knew he could no longer affect. It was almost with compassion that I realized he was more superannuated and hopeless than I. He was no longer gaining the whole world at any price.

"Yes, I know." I moved to leave.

"It's because you know what Ali Agça was really up to in St. Peter's Square that day. It's because you know all those stories and all the others, the ones about the silenced South African bishops, about the missing Stasi files that concern Hitler's relationship with Rome, about the saintly SS mole who sat at the right hand of Pius XII." His face became red and disfigured with withheld rage. "It's because you can place certain prominent archbishops in Ustasha units fifty years ago. It's because you can lay your hands on documents that might reveal why Rome stood by when the Hutu and Tutsi butchered each other, although both sides are all too Catholic. Ah, Father, what you know and what you've done place us, me, in great danger. No member of your organization has ever betrayed its trust. What would you have us do, Father? Forget? Leave you to your passions and your vices, to your studies? Leave you a walking time bomb upon the streets of Rome, presiding over its slip back into heresy and error? No, not while the work of God goes forward."

The last words he nearly spit in my face, then he wheeled and left. I looked about, but no one had been listening. They all sang along with Otis Redding as he sang "I've Been Loving You Too Long," and drank beer and red wine. Outside the brooding statue of Giordano Bruno watched Throckmorton drift into the shadows of the Via Cancelleria. A cold dread touched me then as I rushed out across Rome to my small rooms in the Piazza Eustachio. I was aware of no one following me, but the game was up, they would know by now where I lived and worked. My only thought was for this small work of history.

I look out over the strange steeple of San Eustachio, the stag's head with full rack of horns and a cross growing from its forehead. Under that sign I finish this work. Three packages for you, Dominic, in three envelopes bearing the address of a secret library of the forbidden. Henry Throckmorton, oddly, gave me the courage to finish it. So often, in these last painful months of exile among the proud and worthy citizens of Rome, have I been seen wandering its streets muttering what Leonardo muttered in the margins of his notebooks so many years ago, in another exile: *Tell me if anything ever was done.* Tell me, Dominic, if anything ever was done. True, my small conversion has perhaps helped the cause of Mary, and through her the cause of peace goes forward. Perhaps the winds blow in that direction, Marian devotion leading us back to the true understanding of the feminine wellspring of spirituality I now sometimes glimpse in a dream or a meditation, unworthy as I am of such glimpses. Dominic, it is all filled with contradiction, and the only first step is to lose the way. Throckmorton says that I know too much, I know that I know nothing at all. How little knowledge it takes to threaten this world, how little heart and courage it takes to make one an enemy, a possessor of dark secrets that hound the world into violence. If, for such secrets and for such little courage and with such weak love, I have threatened the established powers of my religion, I can only accept their death as a small joke on power. Perhaps, even under the great pain he felt, the flames licking at his legs, choking the life from his lungs, Giordano Bruno was aware, too, of the small joke we share.

Dominic, tell me if anything ever was done. History seems to coil around and around itself striking and striking at its own tail. I have awakened from a stained and brittle book about the Crusades to hear the bells of the same twelfth century toll again and again. I have walked these streets that bear the scars of a dozen sacks, where Jews in recent memory were torn from their houses and killed, where the stones of the Colosseum and the Forum fall into ruin and reappear over and over again. The barely drowned cries of the early Christians, turning into unheard cries for mercy that rattle down the medieval and Renaissance streets, gather into the modern shouts in South America, in Africa, in Ireland, in the ruins of Yugoslavia. I knelt in one half moment of ecstasy on a nearly deserted beach half a world away and my life was changed. How can those who claim spiritual power in this world have avoided even that much epiphany?

I now watch the dawn rising over the streets of Rome, over the Palatine, the Campidoglio, over the Pantheon. In a few moments everything will be illumined, will be given new breath and life. I have one devious ploy left to ensure that these packages reach you, Dominic. In them, perhaps you will hear only a few bones rattling in an ill wind. In them perhaps you will hear only the rasping growl of the beast, and behind it perhaps the faint echo of my true nature, which has pursued me and finally overtaken me. The beast of my dreams, Dominic, the beast of my dreams.

EPILOGUE

I received these packages from the hands of the postman and carried them back with me through the snow to my small apartment. I read them that night, sitting up near the fireplace with a bottle of wine and a cheap cigar. They had taken about a week to reach me. The next day, a Friday, I called the library and talked to Father Selvaggio. Gabriel had been missing for two days. His rooms had been ransacked, but there was no sign of blood, and no one in the building had heard or seen anything strange. I tied the envelopes in a bundle and set them on the dining room table. I made myself some coffee and sat and stared and thought for a long time. I lit another cigar and smoked it until the ash nearly burned my fingertips.

The morning was cold and bleak. I wrapped the package in three or four layers of newspaper and put them in an old leather case, one of my few remaining priestly possessions. I got in the car and drove toward Preggio, turning up a crushed rock road a few kilometers from there. At the top of the hill was a stone house Gabriel and I helped restore for some crazy Americans who thought they could make money renting an old farmhouse to rich German tourists. The house had been deserted, with a forlorn *Vendesi* sign posted at the bottom of the hill. For some reason I had kept a key to the place. Perhaps, like so many things in my life, I didn't keep it, but had just failed to throw it away.

I took the bag, a small mason's hammer, and a bucket of sand mixed with cement, and let myself into the house. It smelled of mold and rotting onions. It smelled of abandonment and foolishness. I went over the wall Gabriel had built, the wall I had said looked as if a wild animal had built it. It didn't take long to hammer a hole in the wall. Then I hammered angrily at the next course of rock, the older wall behind. I scraped and carved until there was a space large enough to put the leather case in. Then I replaced the stones, careful to match the color and texture of the mortar. I lit another cigar and admired and criticized the job.

So Gabriel had taken that Beguine poem seriously, and it had set him on a path. I, on the other hand, have given up trying to find a purely spiritual path. That is all nonsense. And perhaps I did him some small disservice. But what the hell, putting one stone on another soon makes a wall. And perhaps behind walls things are hidden. So the hell with it. I paused a moment more and then I left for Rome.

Father Selvaggio gave me the address of Gabriel's flat and a spare key he had locked in a drawer. I walked over to it. The *carabinieri* had been there by then and had found no clues. I found no clues either. I did find Jenny's phone number, however, which I folded up and put in my wallet. I walked to the Piazza Eustachio, wandered up the Corso and into the Campo dei Fiori. The flower and fruit sellers had wound up their awnings and pulled their carts into the alleyway. The brooding statue of Bruno dominated the piazza as a street cleaner made slow sweeps around the square. I searched the face under the cowl for some kind of message, but it was enigmatic at best. I walked past the statue, up the street filled with contented Romans going about their business. I hurried past them, as though I were being led, crossed the Arenula and, almost running, found myself before the Teatro Marcello. I was sweating and gasping for air from fear and presentiment, not from exhaustion. There were two or three *polizia municipale* cars parked at odd angles at the end of the Via Portico d'Ottavia. A small crowd had gathered, pressing their faces against the wire fence, straining to see something in the ruins below. I pushed my way rudely through them. Down in the ruins, two white-jacketed attendants were putting the body of a man onto a stretcher. I recognized the tall, thin form, intense and disappointed yet somehow powerful even in death. It was the lifeless body of Father Gabriel D'Amato.

I wept then and I have wept much since, sitting alone in his rooms, a middle-aged man feeling lonely for the first time in his life. I had never felt it before, I who have always pushed loneliness away with mad projects. Perhaps I was only feeling the loneliness of the man who had barely occupied these austere rooms. My God, he had only one coffee cup and one wine glass—how much more lonely can you get, not even to imagine a guest, not even to allow for the possibility?

And yet I knew he had felt love and desire and passion, and the body he left was not the same as that of the man half starved with ambition I had met years ago in the Abruzzi.

I left his rooms and went to the Library of Forbidden Books to tell Father Selvaggio that Gabriel was dead. I found him behind a huge volume of the Inquisitorial transcripts of Joan of Arc. He looked up when he saw me and a wan smile crossed his face. "Ah, Dominic," he said. "Strange, all his heroes and heroines were burned at the stake. By their own hierarchies, for largely imagined offenses. Such a waste of talents, but then the hierarchy is so ignorant of scripture, don't you think? The *polizia* just left, after nearly ransacking his desk and asking me endless impertinent questions."

"Did he ever mention a Sir Henry Throckmorton?"

"Dominic, you are not suited for the role of a detective. Too blunt, I fear, too angry."

I laughed. "The cause of my own problems with the hierarchy. Luckily, I kept no secrets from them. Being a peasant at heart has its advantages."

"A few I might imagine. Peasants always go to bed tired, sleep soundly, and awaken at dawn. No, Gabriel never mentioned him to me. Our pursuits were more scholarly and arcane. He seemed to get keen on the Vestal Virgins toward the last and he read with great interest all the Inquisitorial investigations of apparitions of the Virgin. Of course, until Lourdes and Fatima, records of apparitions had nearly ceased, the Inquisitors being rather firm of hand with the claimants."

"They were usually beaten or publicly humiliated, weren't they?"

"That was quite enough discouragement. After a while, the devout held their tongues. Why he was interested in these matters, Gabriel never shared with me. Usually, I am a little embarrassed to say, he would ask questions and listen to my rather lengthy and digressive answers. The Vestal Virgins. Giordano Bruno, and Renaissance magic. Rosicrucianism. I am an old man, Dominic. And though I have always been pleased with this life, still, as time goes on, fewer and fewer seem interested or cursed with one germ of curiosity. Gabriel was infected in his own way and I so enjoyed talking. Savonarola, Bruno, Joan. My God, *he* wasn't burnt, was he?"

"Apparently not. The postmortem will not be ready until tomorrow. No one else came here looking for him before his death, did they? No one else knew, in the Church I mean, that he was here."

"No. This is a tiny island where human contact is rare and usually a disappointment. Books are keener company, with predictable defects and a uniformly musty odor. The only oddity was his interest in the Vestals. They died out about the time of Constantine, the oldest and the last rite of ancient Rome to die out. A dead end, Dominic. A very dead end." His small black eyes gazed past me and the pallor of his parchment skin deepened, and he was lost in a solitary discussion already taking place in a very remote past.

I wandered for a while through Rome. I am not a scholar, I think I am finally a stonemason. I went from place to place admiring the stonework, the immense undertakings that consumed the sweat and life of thousands. I tried to read the walls, the confident palaces of the Renaissance, designed by the best and paid for with gold earned suitably far away in the past, to acquire a kind of indulgence. The enigma of the Pantheon. My God, who were these masons, these geniuses of cement and brick? The massive columns, the bronze doors. It exhausted me.

I sat for a while in Santa Maria Sopra Minerva. I admired its Gothic vault and had a somewhat stilted conversation with Catherine of Siena. Since her head and thumb were in Siena, the conversation was somewhat one-sided. She had made the mistake of dying in Rome and it took a number of bishops and curial secretaries years to decide how to carve the poor girl up. Since she had helped reunite the Church, they could have left her in one piece.

My thoughts were always like this in Rome, irreverent and lacking in awe for the great procession of history. As I said, I am a peasant, and with each stone wall I build, a little of the foolishness and insanity falls away. As the years have ground on, I have less and less time for the niceties, any niceties. I have lost the desire to change my fellow man. I studied the Beguines, and Zen, and a smattering of everything else. But I don't have a scholar's zeal either. Lately I have one question for everything: Will it make a better wall? Will it stand up to the stress, to the elements? Like I said, a peasant.

I identified the body and claimed it after a tremendous amount of trouble. Gabriel had died of heart failure. But then we all die of heart failure, don't we? There was too much of this and that in his blood, but no apparent puncture wounds. I provided a name, but what caused all the trouble at the police department, what detained me for four or five hours in that dreadfully huge but claustrophobic building, was that nothing in his rooms, nothing on his body, and nothing supplied by Father Selvaggio could pinpoint his identity. The Vatican, of course, was no help and I doubt if his fingerprints actually appeared anywhere on earth after his superiors had finished their house cleaning. I supplied them with a name and, after it became clear I would provide them with nothing more, they issued a death certificate which said little or nothing and released the body to me. So, what the hell, I say, ashes to ashes, dust to dust. I went back to the morgue with a handful of cigars the next day. The medical examiner was reluctant to talk, but they were excellent cigars.

"Your friend's death was not inconsistent with sodium morphate poisoning. Doesn't leave much trace, appears as a massive heart attack. But this man was not scheduled for a heart attack. Good condition for his age actually." He puffed thoughtfully on a cigar. "I wouldn't raise the possibility except we see sodium morphate here now and again. He was dressed as a priest and there were only a few bruises on his body, so there was no reason to make a case of it. At least that was the message I received."

"What do you mean?"

"On such slender evidence I cannot open an investigation on my own authority. My superiors, after a few hours of deliberation during which they made certain discreet inquiries, decided not to proceed."

"Why didn't they proceed?"

"He was a priest, but the Vatican had no record of him. There was no identification on the body. From the police report, he had been dead for about twelve hours when he was found by an elderly insomniac walking his dog. End of evidence. It is strange and leads one to think perhaps there are traces of professionalism here. Yet silence from the Vatican. Stranger still. When a priest is murdered, he usually becomes a martyr to something or other, a candidate for future sainthood. Silence. So the case is closed. Between the two of us, it is rumored the decision not to investigate was made by the highest echelons, the highest." He brandished his cigar for emphasis and I retreated. Case closed.

I had his body cremated, which in Rome took a little wheedling and a lot of bribery. But in the end I had an urn in which, after a few more bribes, I felt reasonably sure were the remains of Father Gabriel D'Amato. I didn't accept any nonsense about ashes. I knew that there would be no ashes really, but mostly bone fragments; so I did not end up with an urn exactly but a small casketlike box. I paid a mason I knew to grind Gabriel's bones into powder under the great stones of his cement grinder, two half-ton stones that turn in unison and pulverize whatever is beneath them. I have become thorough in my advancing years.

I was left with about a kilo of pulverized bone. One night, after even the drunks had vanished, I scattered it at the foot of the statue of Giordano Bruno. Then, privately and for a considerable time, I did what Caravaggio had done after Bruno was burned three hundred and some years earlier. I got drunk and stayed drunk for a few days. Then I cleaned up the cigar butts, the empty bottles, shaved, put on a clean shirt, and called Jenny.

After introducing myself and stating who I was, she said, "He's dead isn't he? They found him."

"Yes" was all I could say without choking.

She invited me over and I went. The sun shone brilliantly and made my head hurt. What the hell, I'm getting too old for this.

Jenny was as beautiful as Gabriel had described, perhaps more. And as innocent in her way. "It didn't go well, you know, our last meeting. I was pissed off, I guess I was a little sprung on whoever he was, but that was the problem. Who was he?"

"I thought he told you?"

"He did . . . confess to me, if you can believe that."

"I can believe it."

"I just didn't, don't get it. He confessed to me, who has no religion, when there are a thousand confessors, a thousand confessionals within a stone's throw of here."

"*I* understand."

"Then tell me."

"The one thing he didn't want was *their* forgiveness," I said. We stood a few feet away from each other. The sadness overwhelmed any need for pleasantries. Jenny shrugged and tears appeared and ran down her lovely cheeks, tears she made no move to brush away.

"I thought he was maybe someone else."

"Actually I think you did come to know him."

"But he wasn't who he said he was."

"But then really none of us are."

"That's not true. You are exactly who you seem to be."

"That's different."

"No."

"Jenny, can I tell you a story?"

"Of course you can . . . Dominic."

"There was this guy, sort of a teacher, who took his students to a fair. At the fair, there was this arcade where you could shoot at tin ducks with a small rifle. You know the kind. Well, this teacher got his students around him and he took aim with the rifle and shot high and erratically, nearly shot the cap off the guy running the game. Everyone laughed. I mean he was the teacher. He was always supposed to be in control. But he turns to them and says, 'That was the *true believer* shooting, he's so sincere and otherworldly, he is out of touch with the nature of the world and misses badly.' The students look at each other and kind of shrug their shoulders.

"The teacher takes up the gun again and this time the shot is low into the bales of hay under the targets. Again they laugh. 'He's just covering for his lousy aim,' they think. He just says, pointing toward the row of ducks, 'That is the *corrupter of religion*, in too much of a hurry and distracted by greed, ambition, hypocrisy. He can't see beyond his assumptions about the nature of the world and misses badly.' The students are quieter now, kind of looking at each other saying, 'Who is this guy?'

Finally, he takes up the gun one more time and, firing rapidly, knocks down the whole row of ducks in a flurry of shots and the rattling of tin. The students are astonished. The teacher puts the gun down and starts to walk away. They follow behind him. 'Who was that?' they shout. 'Who was that?' The teacher just keeps walking, deep in thought. At the end of the street they stop him with their demand. 'Who was that who knocked down the row of ducks, what kind of religious was he?'

" 'Oh,' the teacher replied, 'that was *me.'* And kept walking."

Jenny came over to me and kissed me on the forehead. "I don't understand a damn word," she said, "but thanks."

"What the hell," I replied, holding her against me. "What the hell."